When Silence Falls

SHIRLEE MCCOY

Steeple
Hill®

Published by Steeple Hill Books™

STEEPLE HILL BOOKS

Steeple
Hill®

ISBN 0-373-87354-9

WHEN SILENCE FALLS

Copyright © 2006 by Shirlee McCoy

www.SteepleHill.com

Printed in U.S.A.

My soul waits in silence for God only; from Him is my salvation. He only is my rock and my salvation, my stronghold; I shall not be greatly shaken.

—*Psalms* 62:1–2

To Kitty, Melissa and Lynde McCoy.
Good friends are hard to come by.
I'm glad to count you among mine.

To every mother who has ever longed for a
few moments of precious silence—may you find
joy in the music of your children's laughter and
pleasure in the symphony of their voices.

And to Caleb whose world is like mine—
filled with dragons, princesses, danger and
intrigue—and who is never afraid to be
the person God made him to be.

ONE

Piper Sinclair knew a bad thing when she saw it, and right now she was seeing it. A dozen ladies, all in various colors and styles of spandex, sat on bamboo mats staring with undisguised adoration at a woman whose banal smile set Piper's teeth on edge. A whiteboard at the front of the room stated the purpose of the meeting— "Love Yourself to Weight Loss." On either side of the whiteboard, long candle-laden tables sent up a steady stream of vanilla-scented air.

"Forget it. I've changed my mind." Piper did a U-turn and tried to exit the room, but Gabriella Webber blocked her retreat, her sweet, wouldn't-hurt-a-fly face set in mutinous lines.

"You can't change your mind. You promised."

"I wouldn't have if you'd told me what this seminar was about."

"I did tell you what it was about."

"You said a weight-loss meeting. You didn't say New Age mumbo jumbo." The words were a quiet hiss, but from the look on Gabby's face, Piper might as well have shouted.

"Shhhhh! Dr. Lillian will hear you."

"I'm barely whispering."

But the slim, smiling woman was hurrying across the room as if she had heard the exchange. "Welcome, ladies. I'm Dr. Sydney Lillian. Please, have a seat. We'll be ready to begin in just a few minutes."

Piper wanted to tell the doctor she wouldn't be staying, but Gabby was staring at her with such hopeful pleading she didn't have the heart to walk out.

"Thank you, Dr. Lillian. Come on, Gabby. Let's find a seat." Piper chose a mat close to the back of the room and sat down.

Gabby lowered herself onto a mat a few feet away, then leaned over and grabbed Piper's arm, her dark eyes brimming with excitement. "I can't believe we're really doing this. If this class works as well as it's supposed to, I'll be slim and trim by Christmas. Just in time to find a New Year's date."

"Gabby…" But what could Piper say? That losing weight wouldn't help Gabby find Mr. Right? That Mr. Right didn't exist? That all Piper had ever found were a lot of Mr. Wrongs, all gussied up to look like what they weren't? "You'll have a New Year's date whether you lose the weight or not. You always do."

"I know. I just want this year to be different."

Meaning Gabby wanted commitment, love, marriage. All the things women approaching thirty typically wanted. All the things Piper had decided she could do without. She smiled anyway, patting Gabby's arm. "It will be."

"I hope you're right." Gabby sighed and settled back onto her mat.

Piper's bamboo mat was uncomfortable, and the strange affirmations the class was forced to say made her feel even more so. *I love my belly. I love my hips.* Since when did one need to affirm affection for each and every body part in order to lose weight? By the time the forty-minute session wound to an end, Piper was ready to ask for a refund on her money *and* her time.

"Are there any questions before we adjourn?" Dr. Lillian's voice was like warm honey, but her eyes were cold.

Piper started to raise her hand and got an elbow to the ribs for her effort.

"Don't you dare." Gabby hissed the warning, her eyes shooting daggers.

Piper grinned, shrugged and let her hand drop.

Another woman—a plump blonde with a pretty face and striking blue eyes—raised her hand. "Dr. Lillian?"

"Yes, Piper?"

Despite her gut-level dislike of the woman, Piper felt a twinge of sympathy for Dr. Lillian as the blonde's cheeks stained pink and a frown line appeared between her brows. "I'm not—"

She never had the chance to finish. One minute scented candles and soft music created an atmosphere of gentle serenity, the next, a dark blur raced into sight. A man. Medium height, wearing jeans, a faded T-shirt and a mask. Carrying a gun. A gun!

He grabbed the blonde who'd moments before been pink with embarrassment or anger. Now she was pale as paper, her eyes wide with fear.

Someone screamed. Others took up the chorus.

"Enough!" The gunman shouted the order, the silence that followed immediate and pulsing with terror.

"That's better. Now everyone just stay put and you won't get hurt." He inched toward the door, his arm locked around the blonde's neck, his pale yellow-green eyes staring out from behind the ski mask. Crocodile eyes. And like a crocodile, he had no intention of letting his prey escape alive.

The thoughts flashed through Piper's mind, demanding action. She took a step toward the man. "Let her go."

A mouse could have made more noise.

She tried again. "Let her go. Before you make more trouble for yourself."

His reptilian gaze raked over Piper and dismissed her as no threat. Still, the gun he held never wavered. He kept it pointed toward the group as he took one step after another, slowly, inexorably pulling his victim to the door. Ten steps and he'd be there. Nine.

The long sleeve of his T-shirt hiked up around his forearm, revealing a snake tattoo that coiled around his wrist and up toward his elbow. The deep greens and reds of the serpent seemed to undulate, the gold eyes almost exactly matching the eyes of the gunman. Hard. Evil.

The other women must have sensed the same. Each was frozen in place, eyes fixed on the gun as if staring hard enough would keep it from firing.

Eight steps. Seven. Soon he'd pull the woman out the door and into the parking lot. He'd disappear, the woman with him.

Six.

The smart thing to do would be to wait until the man walked outside and then call for help. It's what Piper's brother Jude would expect her to do. A New York City cop, he knew the best way to respond in a crisis, and he'd drilled her on everything from natural disasters to hostage situations.

Five. Four.

The blonde's eyes were wide with terror, begging someone, anyone, to stop what was happening. Piper couldn't ignore the plea. She stepped forward again, praying for wisdom and for help. "Hey, you're holding her too tight. She can't breathe. She's turning blue!"

The hysteria in her voice was real, and the blonde did her part, moaning, dropping her weight against the arm that held her. The gunman glanced down and that was the chance Piper needed. She leaped forward, raising her leg in a roundhouse kick she'd been practicing for months. Hard. Fast. To the wrist. Just the way her other brother, Tristan, had taught her. The gun flew from the man's hand, landing with a soft thud on the floor a few feet away. Piper dove for it, her fingers brushing against metal just as a hand hooked onto her arm and threw her sideways.

She slammed into a table, her head crashing against the wall, candles spilling onto the table and floor. Stars shot upward in hot, greedy fingers of light.

"Fire!" Gabby's scream cut through Piper's daze and she blinked, focusing on the gauzy curtains now being consumed by flames.

All around her the room echoed with noise—women calling to one another, feet pounding on the floor, an alarm screaming to life. Dr. Lillian stood amidst the chaos, calmly speaking on a cell phone.

"Piper! Come on, we've got to get out of here." Gabby grabbed her arm and pulled her toward the door.

"Where's the guy with the gun? The woman?"

"Gone. He let go of her when you kicked the gun out of his hand. I think you might have broken his wrist."

The thought made Piper light-headed. Or maybe it was the knock on the head she'd gotten. Whatever the case, she felt dizzy and sick. "I wasn't trying to. I just wanted him to drop the gun."

"Well, he did. But he picked it up again before he ran. Now stop talking and move faster."

Outside, daylight had faded to blue-purple dusk, the hazy mid-July heat humid and cloying. People hugged the curb of the parking lot, staring at the smoke billowing from the three-level brownstone that housed Dr. Lillian's practice. In the distance, sirens wailed and screamed, growing closer with each breath. Soon Lynchburg's finest would arrive. If God was good, and Piper knew He was, Grayson wouldn't be with them. The last thing she needed, or wanted, was her oldest brother's raised eyebrow and overburdened sigh.

What she needed, what she wanted, was to walk away. To leave the burning building and the crying, gasping blonde and shell-shocked, spandex-clad women behind, go home and forget any of this had ever happened. But just as Jude had taught her to be cautious and Tristan had taught her to fight, Grayson had taught her responsibility. She was here for the duration. No matter how fervently she wished otherwise.

She sighed, moved into the crowd of people and waited for help to arrive.

Cade Macalister heard the sirens as he pulled out of Lynchburg Medical Center. He ignored them. Or tried.

"Well?" Sandy Morris didn't need to say more. Cade knew exactly what she was thinking.

"No."

"The sirens are close. It won't take long to get the scoop and shoot a few pictures." A reporter for the *Lynchburg Gazette,* Sandy was the wife of Cade's best friend. She was also seven months pregnant.

"No."

"Come on, Cade. What can it hurt?"

"It can hurt a lot if your husband finds out."

"Jim won't mind."

Cade snorted and pulled over as an ambulance sped by.

"They're heading toward the historic district. Something big's going on. See those police cruisers? You know some of the guys on the force. They'd probably—"

"You need to be home in bed, resting. Jim will never forgive me if you go into preterm labor while he's away."

"I'm fine. The doctor just said so."

"Three hours ago you thought you were in labor."

"And I was wrong. This *is* my first, you know. Come on, Cade. You've got your camera, right? We'll get the scoop. Then you can bring me home."

"Sorry, but I'm on duty tonight. I was supposed to be in Lakeview an hour ago."

"Why didn't you say something? I could have found someone else to hang out at the hospital with me."

"I didn't want you to have to find someone else. Besides, another officer is filling in for me until I get there."

"I wish you'd told me. Oh, wait, I get it. Jim talked you into babysitting me while he was out of town, didn't he?" Her voice was sharp, a frown line between her brows.

"Jim didn't have to talk me into anything. We're friends, Sandy. What was I supposed to do? Tell you I had to work and leave you at the hospital alone?"

She shook her head, brown curls sliding against her cheeks. "Ignore me. I've been a bear lately. Go ahead and drop me off at home. I'll miss the story of the century, but I can get the information tomorrow. Better late than never."

Cade rolled his eyes. He knew the score. He'd been friends with Jim for most of his life and with Sandy for the eight years since she'd met and married his friend. The pout, the pretense of agreeing with Cade's plan, they were both part of an act designed to get what she wanted. They worked every time. "You're a pest, you know that?"

"Jim's been telling me that for years."

"Well, he's been right." But Cade turned left at the next light, following a police cruiser and the high-pitched whine of sirens.

"Look! Something's burning!" Sandy's excited cry filled the car, her finger barely missing Cade's nose as she pointed toward thick black smoke that hung above the buildings a few blocks away. A fire truck screamed a warning and raced by Cade's SUV. Before he could pull in behind it, an ambulance roared past. Sandy was right. Whatever was happening was big. Cade's fingers itched to grab his camera, to shoot pictures of the emergency vehicles, the people standing in frozen silence in parking lots and on sidewalks. Fear. Excitement. Cade could read it all in their faces, and he knew he could capture it on film.

Adrenaline pounded through him, urging him to step on the gas and head into the fray. During his years as a crime-scene photographer for the military police, he would have done just that. Time and experience had tempered him. He glanced at Sandy, saw his own urge to move reflected in her face. Too bad. There was no way he was taking her with him.

He pulled into a convenience store parking lot, turned to his passenger. "If you step foot out of this car, I'll burn any pictures I get at the scene. Stay put and the *Gazette* gets first dibs on them."

"Wait a minute—"

"Take it or leave it."

"Take it." Sandy huffed back into her seat, a scowl pulling down the corners of her mouth.

Cade ignored the show, parked the car, grabbed his Nikon off the back seat and pushed open the door. The acrid scent of smoke burned his throat and nose as he made his way along the sidewalk. Up ahead, police cars blocked the road and two officers directed the rerouted traffic. Cade recognized one of them and strode toward him. "Matt! What's up?"

Matt Jenkins turned and glanced at Cade's camera. "You shooting pictures for one of the newspapers?"

"Lynchburg Gazette."

"Thought maybe you were here as a cop."

"I haven't been a cop in a while."

"That's not what I hear."

"What do you hear?" Cade lifted his camera, took a shot of the cruisers blocking the road.

"I hear you're back in uniform. Working in Lakeview."

"Part-time. Just for the summer."

"Part-time. Full-time. Doesn't matter. A cop's a cop."

"Maybe so. You know what's going on?"

"Attempted kidnapping. Fire started during the woman's escape."

"Did you get the perp?"

"Not yet. We've got witnesses, though, so who knows? You can go on through. Must be five news trucks there already."

"Thanks." Cade worked his way toward the scene, scanning the crowds that lined the street, shooting pictures as he went. Just a few would have captured the essence of the moment—the fear and excitement of the crowd, the smoke pouring from the building, ambulances and fire trucks with lights still flashing, news crews pressing toward the scene. Cade was more interested in capturing something else.

"You think he's here?" The voice was familiar, and Cade turned to face Jake Reed, sheriff of Lakeview and Cade's boss as of a week ago.

"Statistically, the chances are good."

"True, but I'm not asking about statistics, I'm asking what you think. Is the perp hanging out in the crowd, or has he already flown?"

"He's here." Cade lifted the camera again, his attention on the people milling about.

"I'm thinking the same. Keep shooting while we walk."

Cade did as he was asked, snapping a shot of Jake

and the crowd behind him. "You're a long way from home, sheriff. Did Lynchburg PD call you in?"

"A friend's sister was on the evening news and he asked me to come check on her. What about you? I thought you were at the hospital."

"A false alarm. It only took three hours to figure it out."

"Glad to hear it wasn't anything serious."

"Me, too. And since it wasn't, I'd be happy to report in tonight." *Desperate* to report in was more apt, but Cade doubted Jake needed to know that.

"We could use another officer." Jake gestured to a group of women standing near an ambulance. "Can you get a couple of pictures of those ladies?"

"Sure."

"And the crowd behind them."

Cade lifted the camera and took several pictures as he moved closer, the lens bringing the group into stark focus. A few women huddled together, soot and tears streaking their faces. Others stared hollow-eyed at the burning building. Shock. He'd seen it too many times not to know what it was. Only one of the women looked animated—a short blonde whose hands danced as she spoke to a uniformed police officer.

She glanced Cade's way as he and Jake approached, her gray eyes wide and thickly lashed, the band of black around her irises giving her an other-worldly look. Cade knew those eyes. Memories flashed through his mind—Seth Sinclair and his three brothers, two of them with the same wide, gray eyes. Their sister—small, always talking, always moving. Always in trouble. Piper. An odd name for an odd kid. Only she wasn't a kid anymore.

Dressed in faded sweatpants and a bright pink T-shirt, her blond hair pulled back in a ponytail, she looked calm, despite the chaos around her. The police officer said something to her and she nodded, lifting thick, straight bangs away from her forehead and revealing a deep blue bruise. Then she gestured to the livid welts along her arm.

Piper Sinclair might not be a kid anymore, but apparently she hadn't outgrown her penchant for finding trouble. Cade could only hope the Lynchburg police would have an easier time of protecting her than her brothers had had while she was growing up.

TWO

Piper was in the middle of explaining for the fifth time the roundhouse kick she'd used to disarm the kidnapper, when Jake Reed stepped up beside her. Sheriff of the small town where she lived, and a friend of Piper's brother Grayson, he was here for one reason and one reason only—to check up on her. Obviously, Grayson had put him up to it.

She might have been annoyed if she hadn't been so glad to see a familiar face.

"Everything okay here, Piper?" Jake's voice was smooth and firm.

"Fine. I was just telling Lieutenant Bradley that it really is possible for a woman my size to disarm a man."

"He's having trouble believing you?" Jake speared Bradley with a look meant to intimidate. It might not have worked on Bradley, but Piper was tempted to take a step away.

Bradley just snapped the gum he was chewing

and shrugged. "I'm just trying to get an accurate picture of how Miss Sinclair managed it."

"I think I've already explained. I used a round-house kick. If you don't know what that is, I can demonstrate."

"Not necessary."

"Then I'm free to go?"

"Let me check with Chief Russell. He might want to ask a few more questions before you leave."

"But—"

Jake put a hand on Piper's shoulder and gave it a light squeeze. "I'll go with him. See if I can speed things along a little."

"I appreciate it." And she did. Her head ached, her throat was parched and all she wanted was to catch a ride back to the college with Gabby, get in her car and go home.

"No problem. You might want to call Grayson while you wait. He's been trying to reach you and he's worried."

"I would, but my cell phone battery died."

"You can use mine." The man standing beside Jake held out a phone. He was tall and rangy, his well-worn jeans and black T-shirt a perfect match for the shaggy, overgrown haircut he sported. A camera, cradled in his hand, seemed as much a part of who he was as his brown hair and green eyes.

Something about those eyes sparked a memory, but it flitted away too quickly for Piper to grasp. "Thank you."

"Not a problem." He turned away, taking some shots of the women who were waiting to be questioned.

Jake left, too, following Lieutenant Bradley across the parking lot to a short, balding man.

Which meant it was time to call Grayson. Piper braced herself and dialed his number.

He picked up on the first ring. "Sinclair, here."

"Gray. It's me."

"Piper! Are you all right? I've been worried sick."

"I'm fine."

"Then maybe you can tell me what's going on. A friend of mine called to say you were on the seven o'clock news. Something about a kidnapping."

"I was at a weight-loss meeting—"

"You don't need to lose weight," Gray cut in, the impatience in his voice obvious.

"Gabby—"

"Why am I not surprised? She's been pulling you into her schemes for…"

"Grayson, can I get a word in, here?"

"Sorry. Go ahead."

Piper took a deep breath, forcing back frustration. "Gabby and I were at a weight-loss seminar and some maniac decided to kidnap one of the women. She escaped, but during the scuffle, candles fell into a curtain and set the place on fire."

"Nice condensed version, sis. Now, why don't you tell me the rest?"

"This isn't my phone. I don't want to run up a stranger's bill."

"I don't mind." How the stranger had heard her when he seemed completely engrossed in photographing the scene, Piper didn't know.

She flashed a smile, then turned away, facing the back of the ambulance she'd been leaning against and lowering her voice. "Look, Gray, we'll talk more later. I've got to go."

"Is Jake there?"

"He's talking to one of the officers."

"Can you ask him to call me when he's done?"

"Gray—"

"Piper, Mom and Dad are enjoying the first vacation they've had in years. I'd hate to ruin it by telling them you're in some kind of trouble."

"That's blackmail."

"Whatever works."

"Fine. I'll tell him." She hung up and thrust the phone back at its owner. "Here you go. Thanks again for letting me use it."

He nodded, his gaze too knowing to be comfortable. "I guess Grayson hasn't changed."

"You know Gray?" No wonder his eyes had seemed familiar.

"*Knew.* But not as well as I knew Seth. He and I were too young to hang with Grayson and his buddies."

He grinned and held out a hand. "Cade Macalister."

"Cade? Cade who used to tie my shoelaces together and laugh when I tripped?" Piper squinted, trying to see the scrawny kid with glasses in the scruffily attractive man who stood before her.

"I guess you remember."

"How could I forget? You and my brother spent hours coming up with ways to torture me."

"Self-defense. You followed us around everywhere. It's hard to look cool when you've got a little girl hanging out with you."

Piper laughed, relaxing for the first time in what seemed like hours. "I guess that's true."

"It's definitely true. How is Seth?"

"Good. He's out of the country. We should hear from him early next month. Aren't you a military guy, too?"

"I was. Dad had a stroke a year and a half ago, and I'm helping him out for a while."

"I'd heard about his stroke. How's he doing?"

"Better." Cade's grimace made a lie of the words.

"Ms. Sinclair?" A short, balding man hurried toward Piper, Jake close behind him, their arrival cutting off the questions she wanted to ask.

"Yes?" She turned toward them, her tension suddenly back.

"I'm Chief Russell. Lieutenant Bradley said you gave him your statement. We'll need you to come by the station tomorrow morning and sign it. Other than that, we're all set. You can stop by at your convenience."

"Thanks."

He nodded, gave her a brief smile and moved away.

"I guess I'm free to go. Thanks, Jake. Nice seeing you again, Cade."

"You, too."

She hurried away, feeling the weight of both men's stares as she slid into Gabby's car.

"Finally! I thought they'd never let you go." Gabby's eyes were dark and filled with worry as she put the car in gear and pulled out of the lot. "Are you okay?"

"I haven't decided yet. How about you?"

"Still shaking."

"Me, too."

"I can't believe I talked you into coming tonight. We both could have been killed."

"But we weren't."

"Thanks to you." Gabby turned into the university's parking lot and pulled up next to Piper's GTO. Then turned to face her. "You're a hero. You know that, don't you?"

Piper laughed and pushed the door open. "The only twenty-nine-year-old hero whose brother sends the cavalry to save her."

"Is that what Sheriff Reed was doing there?"

"Yep."

"And the guy that was with him? The cute one with the camera?"

"Cute? Cade Macalister is *not* cute. He's a menace. Or at least he was when we were kids."

"He's cute."

"To each her own." But even as she said it, Piper silently agreed with Gabby's assessment. "Have a safe trip tomorrow, and have fun in Florida." Piper leaned over and hugged her friend.

"Me and my parents are sharing a two-bedroom condo. I don't think fun is going to be possible."

"At least you won't be teaching. That's got to be worth something." Piper stepped out of the car, hitched her purse up on her shoulder. "See you in a month."

She waved as Gabby drove away, then slid into her own car and started the engine. Usually she enjoyed the forty-minute drive to Lakeview, but tonight she felt anxious and worried, each shadow by the side of the road, every car swooping up from behind, a sinister reminder of the attempted kidnapping.

The outcome could have been so much worse. The gun could have discharged as it fell. Someone could have been hurt in the fire. Or killed. The thought brought a wave of nausea, and a cold, clammy sweat to Piper's brow. Gabby had called her a hero, but there was a fine line between heroism and foolishness. Piper had yet to decide if she'd crossed it.

She swiped a shaky hand across her forehead and forced tense muscles to relax. By God's grace no one had been hurt. Piper wouldn't have to live with regrets or recriminations. She needed to be thankful for that, and move on.

Mozart's Fantasy in D Minor was playing on the radio and she cranked up the volume, trying to lose herself in the music, but the images of the kidnapper and his intended victim were etched deep in her mind and she couldn't shake them, no matter how loud the music or moving the score.

By the time she pulled into her driveway, Piper's nerves were on edge, her hands in a death grip around the steering wheel. She sat in the car, eyes fixed on the front door and the golden glow of the porch light.

A tiny bungalow at the end of a dead-end street, the house had once been her great-uncle Marcus's music studio. Now it was Piper's home. In the three months since she'd moved in, she'd never felt anything but comfortable. Now she felt nervous, afraid to leave the safety of the car and step across the shadowy yard.

She scanned the area, looking for a reason for her unease. The house was the same as it had always been—the wide stoop and steeply slanted roof, the portico and bowed windows. But, to the right, thick woods created a sinister blackness. To the left, Mr. Thomas's hulking Victorian spread its excess across a huge, unkempt yard, its hedges and trees overgrown and wild. So many places for someone to hide.

Unfortunately, Piper couldn't sit in the car all night. She shivered, grabbed her purse and stepped out of the GTO, hurrying across the dark yard and up the steps, her heart thundering in her chest.

The living room was to her left as she entered the house. She walked through it into the dining room, setting her purse on the pine table; listening to the silence, feeling the stillness. Everything was as it should be—the soft hum of the refrigerator, the small pile of mail that sat on the table. Yet Piper couldn't shake the feeling that something was different. She turned on her heels, eyeing the room again and still finding nothing out of place.

Leftover nerves from the day's events. That had to be the reason for her unease. Piper walked through the house anyway, checking the morning room that housed the Chickering piano she'd inherited. Then the kitchen, bedroom, bathroom and office. Everything was as she'd left it, and the too-fast tempo of her heart finally eased as she put on a Bach CD and settled in front of her computer. She had term papers to correct for the music theory class she was teaching at Lynchburg University, music scores to choose for her piano students. Both were tasks she usually enjoyed, though tonight neither appealed to her. Instead, her mind returned again and again to the gunman, the pale face of the woman he'd tried to kidnap, the hysterical screams of the other women, the fire.

The shrill ring of the phone offered a welcome distraction from her thoughts, and Piper grabbed the receiver. "Hello?"

"Piper? It's Wayne."

"Hey. What's up?" Surprised, Piper fiddled with a pencil, wondering what had prompted the call. Though Wayne Marshall was a cousin of sorts, they'd been closest during Uncle Marcus's battle with ALS. Since Marcus's death, Wayne had reverted to the more solitary ways he'd exhibited since his mother had married Marcus fifteen years ago.

"I heard the news. Are you okay?"

"I'm fine. How'd you hear?"

"Channel Seven ran a clip about the kidnapping and fire. I saw you standing near an ambulance."

"How did I look?"

"Good, all things considered. Now can we be serious? You could have been killed."

Piper rolled her eyes. After so many years of knowing one another, Wayne still didn't understand her need to make light of difficult situations. "I know, but I'm fine. And so is everyone else who was there."

"And some guy with a gun is on the loose."

"Hopefully not for long."

"'Hopefully' doesn't do a whole lot for me. What are the police saying?"

"They're investigating. As soon as they know something, I will, too."

"I guess that will have to be good enough. We still on for Saturday?"

"Yes. Mrs. James is expecting us at eleven. It sounds like her husband compiled quite a bit of information about Music Makers. She wants me to use whatever I can." Which was good, as Piper planned to make the book she was writing about her uncle's charitable organization the best it could be.

"It's a shame the guy never got to use it himself."

"It is. Mrs. James is devastated by his death. She broke down twice while we were on the phone."

"It's never easy when someone we love dies."

Wayne's words hung between them, the reminder of the loss they'd suffered making them both pause.

Finally, Piper cleared her throat. "Marcus would be so happy about the book."

"He'd be even happier knowing that you were the one putting it together."

"I just hope I do it justice. Miriam is putting an awful lot of money into this—"

"Has anyone ever told you you worry too much?"

"About a million times."

"So stop worrying. The book will be great. I'll see you Saturday." He hung up and Piper leaned back in the chair, staring up at the ceiling. She should have asked Wayne about the antiques again. Three weeks ago he'd promised to go through Marcus's paperwork, see if there were any sales records for three items that were missing from the collection Piper had inherited from Marcus. He had yet to do it, despite the fact that she'd reminded him several times.

She'd have to ask him when she saw him Saturday. For now, she'd do what he had suggested and try to stop worrying. The caramel cheesecake in her refrigerator would go a long way to help with that. She pushed away from the desk, sighing when the phone rang again.

Grayson's number flashed across the caller ID and Piper let the machine pick up.

"Piper, I know you're there."

That didn't mean she wanted to listen to her oldest brother's lecture.

"I'm home. I can be at your house in fifteen minutes."

Piper grabbed the phone. "I'm sorry, so you can skip any lecture you might have planned."

"No lecture, even though you didn't ask Jake to call me and I had to track him down to get the whole story. I just wanted to make sure you were okay."

"I am."

"Good. Now, go check the windows and doors so we can make sure you stay that way."

She mumbled a complaint, but went anyway, knowing Gray was even more of a worrier than she was. "So, why'd you send Jake? I thought for sure you'd be the one running to my rescue."

"I would have been, but Maria and I were in Richmond registering for wedding presents at some swanky place."

"I can't believe you both managed to find the time. What'd you register for?"

"Plates. Forks. A bunch of kitchen stuff I don't even know how to use."

"Does Maria?" The bedroom windows were locked, and Piper stepped out into the hall.

"She says our chef will know what to do with them."

"A chef? I hope I'm invited to dinner often." Piper didn't switch on the light as she moved through the kitchen and into the morning room.

"As often as you like. Not that Maria and I will be there to enjoy the food with you. She works more hours than I do."

"Is that possible?" She reached for the last window in the room, ready to check the lock. Saw something dark move to block the moonlight. Large. A head. Black. No. A mask. She could see the eyes gleaming. Something slammed into the glass, rattling the window.

Piper screamed. Jumped back, tumbling over the piano bench, righting herself. Grayson's voice shouted for her attention, but she was too busy running from the room to listen. There was another jarring thud. She imagined glass shattering, the dark figure climbing through the broken window. Coming after her.

She screamed again. Grabbed a steak knife from the kitchen counter as she flew past. The bedroom. She'd climb out the window if the intruder made it inside the house. She held the phone under her chin as she locked the door, her hands shaking so hard it took three tries. Her palm was slick with sweat and the knife slipped from her grasp, falling to the wood floor with a sharp thud. She didn't bother picking it up. Just hung up on Grayson and dialed 911, her mouth so dry she was afraid she wouldn't be able speak.

THREE

Cade sped down Main Street, took a hard right onto Fifth, his sirens blaring, adrenaline pumping through him and waking him more than the strong, bitter coffee he'd been drinking. He barely braked as he turned left onto Apple Orchard Lane. Dark and lined with large, lush trees, the street offered plenty of hiding places. He searched the area as he pulled up in front of the tiny bungalow at the end of the road. Flanked by woods on one side and an oversize Victorian on the other, it looked like a fairy-tale cottage. Soft light spilled from the front window, illuminating the yard and the vintage GTO that sat in the driveway.

The front door of the house flew open as Cade stepped out of his car, and a woman tumbled out. Five foot three, maybe a hundred and ten pounds, wearing baggy sweats and a bright pink T-shirt. Cade didn't need to see the color of her hair and eyes to know the woman.

He strode forward, caught Piper's arm as she raced off the last step. "Are you okay? Is he inside?"

"Yes and no."

"You're sure?"

"Yes." Her eyes were wide with fear, her teeth chattering.

"Then go back inside. I'll knock when I'm finished out here."

"But what if he's out here?"

"Let's hope he is. I want to have a little chat with him. Go on. Inside." He nudged her toward the three steps that led to the front door, waited until she was locked inside and made his way around to the back of the property. There was no light here, only the silvery glow of the moon reflected on grass and trees. The yard was empty, but he walked the perimeter anyway, flashing his light into the woods, searching for signs that someone had hidden there. Closer to the house he found a patch of matted down grass, but nothing more. He'd dust the windows and siding for prints, though he doubted he'd find anything. Whoever had been here had fled, leaving little of himself behind.

Was it a coincidence that Piper had stopped a kidnapping attempt three hours ago and was now the victim of an attempted break-in? Cade didn't think so. He radioed for dispatch to locate Jake Reed, and then strode back around to the front of the house.

An engine roared through the darkness and headlights illuminated the street. Cade's hand dropped to his gun, then fell away as a silver Jaguar pulled in behind his cruiser, and a lean, hard-built man stepped out. Grayson Sinclair. Even if Cade hadn't known him years ago, he would have recognized the deputy commonwealth's attorney. Well-known by the community and well-loved by the media, his was a face often in the news.

He strode toward Cade, calm, but for the hot anger that shot from his eyes. "Is my sister okay?"

"Yes."

"What happened?"

"Someone was at her back window."

"You've checked out the backyard?"

"Yes."

"Dusted for prints?"

"Doing it now."

"Have you called—"

"How about you go inside and talk to Piper and leave me out here to do my job, Gray?"

Grayson's jaw tightened, his eyes narrowing. "I know you, don't I?"

"Used to. Cade Macalister."

"Seth's friend. Last I heard you were an MP."

"Now I'm a freelance photographer."

"And part-time cop?"

"Reserves."

"I guess Jake needs the help. Things get busy around here when the summer crowd arrives."

"Grayson?" Piper peeked out the front door, her pale face just visible.

"We'll catch up later, Macalister. You okay, Piper?" Grayson's attention turned to his sister, the anger and frustration Cade had noticed well-hidden as he walked up the front steps and disappeared into the house.

Twenty minutes later, Piper's hands were still shaking. She grabbed cups from the cupboard and tried to pour coffee for the three men sitting in her living room. It splattered over the rim, and she muttered under her breath, wiping the spill up and trying again.

"Need some help?"

Her hand jerked. More coffee spilled. She brushed a strand of hair behind her ear and turned to face Cade. "Only if you're better at pouring coffee than I am."

"I can give it a try." He stepped beside her, eased the coffeepot from her hand, a half smile showing off a deep dimple in his cheek. Had it been there when they were kids? If so, Piper hadn't been mature enough to appreciate it.

"You're staring."

Her cheeks heated, but she didn't turn away. "I'm just trying to match who you are now with who you used to be."

"Don't bother. There's not much of the kid left." His words were light, but something in his eyes made her wonder where he'd traveled in the past years, what he'd seen.

Now wasn't the time to ask. Maybe there wouldn't be a time. Four years her senior, Cade had been Seth's best friend. The last time Piper had seen him, he'd been eighteen and getting ready to enlist. Now he was thirty-three. A man who was nothing like the teenager he'd once been.

"You have a tray for these?" He gestured to the cups he'd filled.

"Right here." She set the cups on the tray, then pulled out a package of chocolate chip cookies and piled some on a plate. Before she could lift the tray, it was in Cade's hands and he was leading the way back into the living room where both Grayson and Jake were waiting.

Piper stepped into the room behind him and sensed a tension that hadn't been there when she'd left to make the coffee. She glanced at Jake Reed, who'd arrived soon after Grayson. He looked frustrated and angry, his mouth set in a firm line.

Grayson looked just as angry and just as frustrated. Jaw lined with dark stubble, his short hair slightly mussed, he was as close to unkempt as Piper had ever seen him. He looked up as Piper approached, some of the anger seeping from his gaze. "Coffee. Just what I needed."

Piper grabbed a cup and handed it to him. "Why don't you take it to go? You look like you've had a long day."

"I have. But I'm not going anywhere until I hear what Jake plans to do to keep you safe."

"What do you expect him to do? Put a guard on me twenty-four hours a day?"

"If that's what it takes."

"You know that isn't possible, Gray." Jake's words were calm, with just an undertone of irritation. Obviously, they'd been discussing this while Piper was in the kitchen.

"Possible or not, it's what I want."

"And I wish I could give it to you, but I can't. We don't have enough evidence that Piper's in danger to justify the manpower."

"Evidence? She got knocked around at that weight-loss class. Now someone's tried to break into her house—"

"If he'd wanted to get into the house he would have. Old single-pane glass. Flimsy doors. It wouldn't take much effort to get inside," Cade said, his words interrupting the argument. Piper was sure he'd planned it that way.

She glanced at the door and windows, pictured a masked person breaking in, and shivered.

Grayson nodded. "I think you should come stay with me for a while."

"You've got a one bedroom condo. I'd be sleeping in the living room, and I'd have to come back here to teach piano lessons."

"Then I'll stay here."

"Gray, I'll be fine."

"Maybe. But your brother's right to be worried about you," Cade said, his gaze traveling the room, touching on the windows and the front door. "You don't have a security system, do you?"

"No, I never thought—"

"A dog's a better idea, anyway." Grayson stood and began pacing the room.

"A dog?"

"Sure. They're more effective than a security system when it comes to scaring people away."

"I don't think a dog will fit my lifestyle."

"One of my men brought a German shepherd to the SPCA a few days ago," Jake added, completely ignoring Piper's protest. "Female. Maybe two years old. She was wandering around near the lake. If she hasn't been claimed she'd be perfect."

"Why don't I pick you up after work tomorrow? We can go to the SPCA, see if the shepherd's still there." Grayson paused, his brow furrowed. "Wait. I can't. I've got a dinner meeting."

"That's all right. I'll go myself." Maybe. Though as far as Piper was concerned, Grayson's unavailability was the perfect excuse to *not* get a dog.

"Do you know anything about dogs?" Cade's question caught her off guard, and she shook her head, recognizing the mistake immediately.

She tried to backtrack, think of a good reason why she'd be capable of picking out the perfect guard dog, but came up blank. "I'm sure someone at the shelter will be able to help me."

Apparently Cade wasn't. He leaned forward, his steady, reassuring gaze almost masking the humor that danced in his eyes. "Maybe it *would* be a good idea for one of us to go with you."

"I wouldn't want to put anyone out."

"You wouldn't be. I'm doing a photo shoot at the new medical clinic tomorrow. It's ten minutes away.

Why don't I stop by when I'm finished? We'll go to the shelter together."

"I'm giving a final exam tomorrow. I can't be out."

"It's your early day isn't it, Piper?" Grayson knew it was. Just as he knew she wasn't gung ho about the dog idea. Of course, being Grayson, he focused on the part that coincided with his plans and completely ignored the rest.

"Yes, but I'm not sure—"

"Then it's settled." Cade set his coffee cup down on the tray and pulled a business card from his pocket, flashing his dimple and acting like he had no idea Piper would rather not go to the shelter. "Here's my card, Piper. Call if something comes up. Otherwise I'll be here at two. I'd better get back on patrol." He stepped past Grayson and disappeared into the darkness. Jake followed close on his heels.

"I'm staying the night, and don't even bother trying to talk me out of it," Grayson said as he stepped out onto the front stoop. "I need to talk to Jake. I've got the key. Lock the door. I'll let myself in when we're finished." With that, he was gone, too.

Which left Piper alone, wondering how she'd allowed herself to be railroaded into a trip to the SPCA.

"Men. Can't live with 'em. The end."

She grumbled the words to herself as she snagged a cookie and marched to the linen closet. She was half tempted to make Grayson sleep on the sofa, but since it was only a little longer than a love seat and he was just over six feet tall, Piper thought that would be cruel and unusual punishment.

The curtains in her room were open and she hurried over to close them, her gaze drawn to the branches that swayed in the breeze outside the window. If someone was outside watching the house, watching her, she'd never know it. Not until it was too late.

Maybe a dog wasn't such a bad idea.

She shook her head. No way. Dogs were messy and they stunk. She did *not* want a dog. Then again, she wasn't sure she liked the idea of being alone in the house with a snake-tattooed kidnapper holding a grudge against her. She *knew* she didn't like the idea of Gray sacking out in her house every night. She loved her brother, but he was overprotective and bossy. One night was about all she could take of him.

She tugged fresh sheets onto her bed, her mind racing with a million thoughts, a million worries. She had a lot to do in the next few months. A book to write. Piano lessons to teach. Finals needed to be administered and graded. She had to plan and practice the music for church. Make sure the collection of musical antiques she'd inherited were catalogued, appraised and ready to go on loan to the Lynchburg Museum of Fine Arts. *And* she'd offered to help Miriam plan the exhibit's grand opening to coincide with Music Maker's twenty-fifth anniversary.

What had she been thinking?

She hadn't been thinking. *That* was the problem. She'd been asked and she'd said yes. At the time, she'd really thought she could do it. Now, she wondered if what she'd thought she could do was a little more than what she was capable of.

A few weeks ago Gray had accused her of having superwoman syndrome. Had he been right? *Did* she think she could do everything? Accomplish everything? Did she jump into things without thinking them through? Maybe sometimes. But not now. Now she was thinking. And what she was thinking was that she definitely didn't need a dog complicating her life. She'd call Cade tomorrow and tell him she wasn't going to the SPCA. That would take care of at least one of the problems. Everything else would work out in its time. She hoped.

As Piper finished making the bed, she had the sinking feeling that that wouldn't be the case, that maybe tonight's troubles were only the beginning. She shivered, grabbed the quilt off the end of her bed and walked back out into the living room. Huddled on the sofa, gaze fixed on the door, she could only pray that she was wrong.

FOUR

A night spent tossing and turning on her hand-me-down sofa left Piper feeling groggy and irritable. Fighting Grayson for time in the house's sole bathroom only worsened her mood. By the time she ran out to the car, already five minutes late, a bagel clutched in one hand and a diet soda in the other, her briefcase and purse under her arm, Piper felt like she'd already put in a full day's work.

Grayson looked just as tired as he pulled open the door to his car. "You're meeting Cade here at two. Don't forget."

He didn't ask, and she decided to save an argument and not mention that she planned to cancel. "And you're sleeping at your own place tonight."

"We'll see."

"Gray—"

"We're both running late. Let's discuss it later."

"Why is it that you always say that when we don't agree on something?"

But Grayson was already in his car, waving as he drove away.

Piper shook her head, shoved a last bite of bagel in her mouth and yanked open the door to the GTO. There was no sense being irritated. Grayson was Grayson, determined to have his way in everything. They'd talk. She'd present her view of things. He'd disagree. In the end, he'd do exactly what he wanted.

And tonight he'd be sleeping on the couch.

Classical music was playing on the radio, but Piper needed something different this morning. Contemporary Christian music seemed just the thing to lift her dark mood and she hummed along with familiar tunes as she drove. The sun peeked over the trees, bright orange against the azure sky. It would be a beautiful day. Perfect for hiking near Smith Mountain Lake.

Too bad Piper wouldn't have time for it. She had two classes to teach this morning. Then she'd stop at the police station to sign her statement, call Cade, practice for Sunday's service and then teach piano from five to nine. A full day, but if she kept on schedule, everything should work out fine.

Of course, things never quite turned out the way Piper planned and she wasn't surprised when it took her double the time she'd expected it would to sign her statement at the police station. Nor was she surprised when she arrived home and found an unfamiliar SUV parked in front of her house.

She glanced at the dashboard clock, saw that it

was a few minutes after two, and knew exactly who was waiting. "Perfect."

Piper shoved open the car door and climbed out, her breath catching as Cade stepped out of the SUV. Dark aviator glasses, too-long hair, an easy, comfortable way of moving. A smile that should be outlawed.

And that was something Piper did *not* want to be noticing. She had enough men in her life. One more would just complicate things.

She turned away, yanking her purse from the passenger seat and calling over her shoulder, "Sorry I wasn't here when you arrived. Have you been waiting long?"

"Just a few minutes. I was a little early."

"And I'm a little late." She grabbed her briefcase, shoved the door closed with her hip.

"Rough day?" He pulled the briefcase from her hand, started toward the house.

"I've had worse. How about you?"

"I guess I could say the same. The photo shoot was easy. Dealing with my father, not so easy."

"How is he?"

"Better physically. Mentally is a different story. I thought moving him back here would help. So far, it's just made things worse."

"Have you been back long?" Piper followed him up the stairs to the front door.

"About a month. I…" His voice trailed off. "Your door is open."

"What? It shouldn't be. I locked it before I left this

morning." Her pulse sped up as she sidled close, leaned past Cade's arm and watched as he pushed with one finger and the door creaked inward.

"Go get in the car."

"But—"

"Go. If I'm not out in ten minutes, call for backup." The hard tone of his voice had her moving, hurrying back to her GTO, watching as Cade disappeared inside her house.

Seconds ticked by. Then minutes. She was supposed to wait ten, but Piper didn't think she'd make it five. She grabbed her cell phone, clutched it in her hand, ready to dial 911. Was Cade okay? Should she call for help and then go inside?

Before she could decide, a figure rounded the corner of the house and Piper's heart lurched, settling back into place as she recognized Cade.

She scrambled out of the car, searching his face, trying to determine what he'd found. "Did you see anyone?"

"Nothing. It doesn't look like anything was touched, either. Want to come in and see?"

She did, and followed him into the house.

He was right. Everything looked just the way she'd left it. Her quilt thrown over the couch. A book sitting on the end table. A glass in the kitchen sink. A few crumbs on the counter. In the morning room, the mahogany wood of the piano gleamed in the sunlight that streamed through the window. Piper walked into the office, her bedroom and the bathroom, and found each in order, nothing out of place, nothing missing.

Finally satisfied, she grabbed a soda from the refrigerator, offered one to Cade. "So, what do you think?"

"It doesn't look like anyone was here. The door was locked, just not closed all the way. Is it possible you didn't shut it when you left?"

"No. I shut it." She thought back, trying to remember the moment she'd closed the door. She'd been carrying her purse, briefcase, bagel, soda. "Then again, I was in a hurry and I had a lot in my hands. It could be I didn't pull hard enough and the lock didn't click."

"Or someone was here, but doesn't want you to know it."

"Why? That doesn't make sense."

"Things don't always make sense, Piper. If they did, police work would be a lot easier." Cade took a swallow of soda, trying to decide how much he should say. "Most likely this is exactly what it seems to be—a locked door that wasn't shut tightly enough."

Piper relaxed at his words, the crease between her brows smoothing. "Good. The thought of someone snooping through my house while I'm gone is creepy."

"I agree. Which is why getting a dog is such a good idea."

"About that…" She shifted, turning away to grab a towel and wipe crumbs from the counter. "I'm not sure a dog will fit my lifestyle."

"I guess that's your choice to make."

She glanced over her shoulder, meeting his gaze. "So you're not going to argue with me?"

"No."

"Try to convince me I'm wrong?"

"Should I?"

"I guess not, though every other man in my life would."

"Then it's good I'm not any of the other men in your life."

She smiled for the first time since getting out of her car, her face lighting, her eyes silvery gray. "I'm sorry you came all the way over here for nothing."

"It's not a problem. I was on my way home, anyway."

"Are you close?"

"Just a few streets over. Off of Main Street."

"And you moved in there a month ago? I can't believe I didn't hear anything about it. Usually news spreads like wildfire around here."

"Between my work and Dad's physical therapy I'm gone more than I'm home, so there's probably not much news to spread."

"I can sympathize. I probably wouldn't be home at all if I didn't teach piano lessons here."

"This used to be your uncle's studio, didn't it?"

"I'm surprised you remember."

"How could I forget? Seth had carpool duty the year he got his license. We'd pick you up from school and drop you off here. Then interrupt whatever we were doing to come back and bring you home."

"That's right. I'd forgotten. But now that you mention it, I seem to recall a few very tense car rides." She was smiling again, her face soft with memories, her fingers tapping against the kitchen counter.

She'd grown into her fey eyes and stubborn chin, grown into the gangly arms and legs that had been too skinny when she was a teen. Now, dressed in white slacks and matching jacket, a vivid blue tank top in some silky material beneath it, she looked like the accomplished professional she'd become. A very attractive professional, and Cade wasn't sure he was comfortable with the change.

Nor was he comfortable leaving her alone in the house when his gut said there was more to the open door than there seemed to be.

So maybe now was the time to try a little persuasion.

He straightened, placing his empty can on the counter. "If you're sure you're not interested in going to the SPCA, then I'd better head out."

"I'm sure."

"Good. Too bad for the dog, though."

"What dog?"

"The dog you would have been giving a home to."

Her eyes narrowed, her fingers stilling. "You said you weren't going to try to talk me into it."

"Actually, I said I wasn't going to argue with you, or try to persuade you. And I'm not."

"Then what do you call what you're doing?"

"Presenting the facts."

"And they would be?"

"You're alone in a house at the end of a very secluded street. Your house is about as secure as an open safe in the middle of a den of thieves. Last night, someone came very close to breaking into one of your windows. Today, you came home and found your front door open."

"You said—"

"I said it was probably nothing, but that doesn't mean it was. A dog will serve as a deterrent and an early warning system. If anyone gets within a few hundred feet of the house, you'll know it. You'll have added security and the dog will have the home it needs. Sounds like a win-win situation to me."

For a moment she was silent. Then she shook her head, amusement flashing in her eyes. "You're good. Really good. My brothers would have beaten me over the head with their opinions. Then demanded I do what they wanted. You're just standing there as relaxed as can be, waiting for me to make the right choice for me and for some dog I haven't even met yet."

"Is it the right choice for you?"

"I don't know, but now I feel obligated to check it out." She looked disgruntled, but not altogether unhappy, amusement still dancing in her eyes, her fingers tapping a rhythm on the counter once again.

"Let's head out then."

"Give me ten minutes to change." She started down the hall toward the bedroom, then turned back. "Promise me one thing."

"What's that?"

"You won't let me walk out of there with more than one dog."

He had the nerve to laugh, his eyes, green as the Irish hills his family had come from, sparkling with mirth. "I promise."

FIVE

Piper had known it would come to this—standing in the SPCA kennel, looking at one dog after another and wishing she could adopt them all despite the fact that she knew she didn't want even one. The pitiful little terrier mix that would keep her up all night with its yapping, the black lab mix that looked like it had more energy than brains, the beautiful German shepherd that had been found wandering beside the lake—each in need of a good home. And then there were the rest—barking, yapping, howling, begging for attention. Piper turned in a circle, scanning the long row of cages. "How could I ever choose?"

"The shepherd is beautiful, and it looks like she's had training." Cade stood at the shepherd's cage, eyeing the dog in question.

"Which means there will be plenty of people who want to take her home. I'd rather give a second chance to a dog who probably won't get one."

"Do you mean that?" The SPCA volunteer who had walked them back into the kennel area spoke up, scratching the top of his balding head and shifting from foot to foot.

"Mean what?"

"What you said about giving a chance to a dog that wasn't going to get one?"

It sounded like a question Piper should answer with a loud and firm "no," but she was intrigued, wondering what kind of animal could possibly be so bad it had no chance at all of a home. "I guess that depends on the dog."

The volunteer studied her for a minute, then issued a curt nod. "Come on. This way."

Piper glanced at Cade, who shrugged and gestured for her to follow. They walked past cage after cage, rounded a corner and spotted the biggest dog Piper had ever seen. Huge paws, huge brown head, huge amounts of slobber drooling from his mouth. Obviously, this was the dog no one wanted.

"This is Samson. Purebred Great Dane. A little over a year old. His owner passed away four months ago. No one in the family could keep a dog as big as Sammy, so they brought him here. He's got a great disposition. Loves cats, kids and people in general." The volunteer patted the door of the cage and the dog pressed his head against the metal, perhaps hoping for a scratch.

"Then why is he still here?"

"Samson's been adopted twice and returned twice. Every time he starts to settle in he's uprooted again."

"Poor thing." Piper stepped forward to get a

closer look, stopping when Cade's hand wrapped around her wrist.

He leaned forward, speaking so close to her ear she could feel the warmth of his breath against her skin. "Did you notice he didn't answer your question?"

She had, but as always, the instinct to say "yes, I can do it" overshadowed the voice in her head shouting "no way!"

Only this time she was going to think things through, get all the facts and then decide what she *wanted* to do, not what she felt obligated to do.

She cleared her throat, turned her gaze away from the dog. "What were the reasons Samson was returned?"

The volunteer rocked back and forth on his heels and scratched the top of his head again. "At the first placement we found for him, he broke about a thousand dollars' worth of antique glassware. At the second, he didn't break anything, he was just under his new family's feet and constantly knocking over chairs and lamps."

"I guess a big dog needs a lot of extra room."

"Depends more on the owner than the dog. A young gal like you will have plenty of energy to take Samson for walks, get rid of all his extra energy. Come on and meet him."

Before Piper could protest, he'd pulled a key from his pocket and unlocked the kennel door. The dog rose from his haunches, tail wagging, brown eyes staring into Piper's. If dogs could speak, Piper knew this one would be saying, "Go ahead. Take me home. You won't even know I'm there."

He walked out of the kennel with the volunteer, grinned a big, sloppy doggy grin and sat on Piper's feet.

She couldn't help smiling as she leaned forward to scratch Samson behind his ears. His fur felt warm, smooth and much softer than she'd expected. Maybe taking a dog home wasn't such a bad idea.

She was going to take the dog. Cade could see it in Piper's face—worry, dread and excitement. The dog knew it, too, his giant head pressed against Piper's stomach, his eyes staring straight into hers. A con man if Cade had ever seen one.

Piper rubbed the dog behind its ears. Then she straightened, her ponytail swinging with the movement. Brown fur stuck to the shimmering treble clef symbol on her T-shirt and she brushed it off, a frown line appearing between her brows as she met Cade's gaze. "I guess you're not going to try and talk me out of this."

"You told me not to let you go home with multiple dogs. You didn't say anything about pony-sized ones."

"So, you don't have any opinion about it?"

"My opinion doesn't count. You're the one who's got to live with him."

"I know. And I should probably get a smaller dog. But he's just so…"

"Pitiful?"

"I was thinking sweet." She looked disgruntled as she reached down to pat the dog's head. "My brothers are going to think I'm insane. I can just hear Gray now—*what were you thinking, Piper?*"

"So?"

"You'd have to be the youngest child to under-stand."

"Maybe. But even if I were a youngest child instead of an only, I don't think I'd let my siblings' opinions keep me from doing what I thought was right."

"I don't plan to. I'm just preparing myself for their disapproval." Her voice was light, but there was an undercurrent of something—maybe frustration—lacing the words.

"They won't disapprove. The dog is big enough to scare away the most persistent intruder. Your brothers will appreciate that." He gave in to tempta-tion and tucked a strand of hair behind her ear, letting the silky threads of it slide through his fingers.

Her eyes widened, her face—usually pale porce-lain—tinged pink and she stepped away, the frown line back between her brows. "One way or another, I'm about to find out." She turned to the volunteer and smiled. "What do I need to do to adopt him?"

An hour later they were on their way home and Piper was wondering what she'd gotten herself into. Again. She sighed, pulled the rubber band from her ponytail and rubbed the sore spot at the base of her neck. Talk about tension! Who knew deciding to adopt a dog could be so stressful? At least she had a few days to prepare for Samson's arrival, though she wasn't sure that was even possible. Samson was huge. Her house wasn't. Maybe the SPCA would decide her bungalow wasn't a suitable home for the dog she'd chosen. Piper couldn't decide if that would be a disappointment, or a relief.

"Regretting it already?" The quiet rumble of Cade's voice interrupted her thoughts.

"Not regretting it. Just wondering how I'm going to manage. I work a lot. Travel some. This summer I'll be doing even more of that than usual."

"Yeah? Why's that?"

"I've been hired to write a book about the non-profit organization my uncle founded."

"Music Makers?"

"Yes. There's going to be a huge fund-raising event next December. A twenty-fifth anniversary gala—those are Miriam's words, not mine. The book is going to be given out as a gift."

"Miriam?"

"Miriam Bradshaw. Curator of the Lynchburg Museum of Fine Arts. Friend of my uncle. Longtime supporter of Music Makers. She's got a million hats and wears them all well. If I were half as organized and efficient as her, I'd be happy."

"You seem pretty organized and efficient to me."

She snorted.

"You do."

"Because you don't know me. But that's not the point. The point is, I'm going to be traveling out of state to conduct interviews. Miriam wants the book to be a photo history of Music Makers' service to the community. We've picked one or two people from each year, successful musicians who owe at least some of what they've accomplished to the foundation. We'll get photos of the musician, his or her instrument, then…" What was she doing? Boring Cade to tears, most likely. She'd yet to meet a man who was even vaguely interested in what she did for a living.

"Then what?"

"Put the photos together with my commentary, but I think you've probably heard enough. I'm excited about the project and tend to talk about it incessantly."

"You've got a right to be excited. The book sounds great. Your uncle would have been pleased."

"I know." She fell silent, not sure what else to say, the weight of her uncle's death still heavy on her heart.

She thought Cade might say something comforting, offer the same words she'd heard over and over since Marcus's death. Instead, he reached for her hand and squeezed it, letting her have her silence.

She cleared her throat, forced back her sadness. "It's going to be hard to find someone to pet-sit this late in the season. Everyone already has plans."

"Not everyone."

"You know someone who might be willing to watch Samson?"

"Sure do. My father."

"I thought he wasn't doing well."

"He'd be doing a lot better if he'd stop feeling

sorry for himself." The words sounded harsh, but the concern in Cade's face took the sting out of them.

"You're worried."

"Worried and frustrated. When Dad had his stroke, the doctors weren't sure he'd live. When he survived, they weren't sure how much neurological damage there'd be. Now, he's on the verge of getting back his independence, but instead of pushing for it, he's complaining. Taking care of someone or something else might be just what he needs."

"Do you think he'd agree to it?"

"If I ask him? No. If you ask him? Maybe."

"Then I guess I'll ask him. When's a good time to stop by?"

"Any time you want. Dad doesn't leave the house except for physical therapy sessions. And even that's a struggle."

It sounded like things were a lot worse than Cade was letting on. Piper worried her lower lip, tried to think through her schedule over the next few days. "How about tomorrow evening?"

"That should work."

"Should I invent an excuse for stopping by?"

"We're friends. You don't need any other excuse."

Friends. Good, that's exactly what Piper wanted to be, that's *all* she wanted to be. She'd spent too many years dating men who were more interested in themselves than in her; too many years looking for that elusive dream—soul mate, perfect match, one and only. They were all the same, and none of them existed.

But that was a thought for another time. Piper pushed it aside and got back to the topic at hand. "I'm driving to Richmond tomorrow. Why don't I give you a call when I get back?"

"Sounds good. Are you going to Richmond alone?"

If Piper hadn't grown up with four brothers she might not have heard the change in tone, the shift from easy conversation to intent interest. "No. Wayne is going with me."

"Wayne?"

"Marcus's stepson. You knew Marcus married, right?"

"No. That must have been after I left for basic training."

"Wayne was maybe fifteen when they got married. A bit of a hothead, but not a bad guy. Now he works for Music Makers as a regional account manager."

"And his mother?"

"Theresa passed away a few years back. Cancer. She was a concert pianist. She met Uncle Marcus at a Music Makers fund-raiser."

"And it was love at first sight?"

"That depends on who you ask."

"I'm asking you."

"Then I'd say it was mutual attraction and like interests. Over time those things became love."

"In other words, you don't believe in love at first sight."

"Do you?" Piper turned in her seat, watching Cade's expression.

"I'm open to the possibility."

"Really? I'm surprised."

"Why?" Cade shot a look in her direction, a smile hovering at the corner of his eyes.

"In my experience men like things to be concrete and measurable. Love at first sight is definitely not that."

"Isn't it? I'd say love can be measured. At least by the person experiencing it." He glanced her way again, a half grin curving his lips.

Piper's stomach lurched, her heart skipped a beat and she knew without a shadow of a doubt that Cade was going to be a lot more troublesome now than he'd ever been when they were kids.

SIX

The alarm went off before the sun rose the next morning. Piper slammed her hand down on the snooze button, thought better of it and dragged herself out of bed. She needed caffeine. Now. The hallway was dark and she didn't bother with a light as she moved through it and into the kitchen. The sickly green glow of the oven light shouted the time—five. Way too early to be awake on a Saturday.

Piper shuddered, and yanked open the refrigerator door. There were two cans of soda on the lower shelf and she grabbed one, making a mental note to buy more when she got back from Richmond. She'd need to buy dog food, too. And a bed of some sort. She couldn't expect Samson to sleep on the hardwood floor.

But first things first. She popped open the can, took a swallow and grabbed her Bible and devotional book from the kitchen table, where she'd left them several days ago. A few minutes of quiet time before she began the day should get her started on the right foot. She hoped. Lately, nothing seemed to start her off right. Then again, lately she seemed to be spending less and less time studying her Bible and more and more time thinking about studying it.

She frowned, was still frowning as something moved in the periphery of her vision. Startled, she turned, watching in horror as a dark figure lurched up from behind the sofa. She screamed, dropped the soda, her mind blank of all but one thing—escape.

"Good grief, Piper. That scream could wake the dead."

"Grayson?" Relief made her knees weak and she collapsed onto the chair, her heart still thundering as her brother stepped into the room and flipped on the kitchen light. Dressed in dark green pajamas, his hair standing on end, he looked like he'd been woken from a sound sleep. Which he probably had been.

And he wasn't happy about it. The scowl on his face told the story. His tone echoed it. "You nearly gave me a heart attack skulking around in the dark like that. Why didn't you turn on a light?"

"*I* almost gave *you* a heart attack? At least you knew I was in the house. I had no idea you were here." Her legs were still shaking as she stood up, grabbed some paper towel and started cleaning up spilled soda.

He had the decency to look chagrined. "You're right. I'm sorry. I assumed you knew I was coming, but I should have double-checked."

"Actually, I did think you were coming. When you weren't here by midnight I figured I was wrong."

"I didn't get here until three."

"No wonder you're so grumpy.

"I'm not grumpy. I'm just not a morning person." He scowled again, crossing to the coffeemaker and starting it.

"Be thankful you can go back to sleep. I've got to spend three hours in a car with Wayne."

"I didn't know you had a problem with Wayne."

"I don't. I have a problem with his taste in music."

That made Grayson smile, his eyes flashing with amusement. "Three hours of country western torture. I feel your pain."

"Hey, it's no laughing matter."

"I'll make you some eggs and toast. Plenty of protein. A little carbs. That should fortify you for the experience."

"Thanks, but Wayne's going to be here in an hour and I still need to get ready."

"I'll make the eggs. You get ready. You can eat when you're done. You're going to Richmond, right?"

"Yes, the address is on the fridge. I've got my cell phone if you need to contact me."

"Think it'll be worth the trip?"

It was a question she'd been asking herself since she received Deborah James's phone call. A long commute for something that might not be of any benefit seemed a waste of time. Unfortunately, Piper hadn't had the heart to refuse. "I don't know. The guy was a freelance writer and I haven't been able to track down anything he's written, so we'll see what kind of research process he employed. If nothing else, it'll make his wife happy. She's determined that what he's done not go to waste."

"Anyone ever tell you you're too nice?"

"About as many people who tell me I worry too much." She sighed, grabbed her Bible and devotional book, and retreated to her bedroom.

She tried to read, but the words were a mishmash of letters with no meaning, her mind too full to concentrate. Finally, she closed her Bible and set it aside, ignoring the quiet voice inside that told her she should persist. Maybe tonight, after she finished her errands and stopped by Cade's house, she'd be able to focus. For now, there were just too many other things to do.

A quick shower, a few minutes with the blow-dryer and a minimum of makeup made her feel a bit more positive about facing the day. The dark denim jeans and sleeveless turtleneck she wore were designed for comfort. Piper added a lightweight blazer, pulled her hair back in a loose ponytail and was ready to go.

The doorbell rang as she stepped out of her room, and she hurried into the kitchen. "I'll get it."

"Tell him to come in and eat."

"We don't have time." Though Piper had to admit, the fluffy yellow scrambled eggs Grayson scooped onto a plate looked good.

She ignored temptation, grabbed her purse off the couch and pulled open the front door.

Wayne looked tired, his skin pale in the glaring outside light, his dark hair mussed, his glasses doing nothing to hide the circles under his eyes. "Morning."

"You sound cheerful."

"I am cheerful. My brain just hasn't figured it out yet."

"Eggs might help." Grayson strode across the room, a plate piled high with scrambled eggs held out in front of him. "They're brain food, after all."

"I thought that was fish." Wayne grabbed the plate and headed for the kitchen.

"Wait a minute! You don't have time for that. We have to be in Richmond in four hours. It's a three-hour drive."

"Which gives us an entire hour to spare." Wayne pulled a fork out of Piper's utensil drawer and dug in.

"It would, if we knew for sure we weren't going to get lost trying to find Mrs. James's house."

"Knowing you, you've done the map search, printed out directions and triple-checked the address."

"That doesn't mean we won't get lost."

"You won't. Here. Eat." Grayson thrust a plate at Piper.

"Weren't you just telling me you couldn't cook, Gray?" She grabbed the plate, inhaling a buttery aroma.

"Eggs are it. I don't count toast because I tend to burn it." He dropped a blackened piece of bread on her plate. "What time are you planning to be home?"

"We should be back in town by early evening.

Then I'm running a few errands and dropping by Cade's house to visit his dad. Why?"

"I thought I'd bring Maria by. We're discussing houses. She wants something big and new, I want something older and cozier."

"And you think bringing her here will help her see your side?"

"It can't hurt."

"Then bring her by whenever you want."

"Thanks. You didn't tell me how your dog search went yesterday."

"It went well."

"You liked the shepherd?"

"She was nice."

"And?"

"And I picked a different dog. The SPCA is conducting a home study Monday."

"You're getting a dog? What kind?" This from Wayne, who'd finished his eggs and was piling more onto his plate.

"He's pretty big," Piper hedged, not sure if she wanted to say exactly how big while they were all standing in her tiny kitchen.

"Big is good." Grayson put his plate in the sink, smoothed down his hair. "Add an alarm system and your security goes up a hundred fold. I'll call Micah Jefferson later today. He put in Maria's system."

Piper thought about arguing, but what good would it do? As her mother often told her, sometimes it was better to go with the flow than to fight the current.

"Give him my cell-phone number. I'll set up a time to meet him. Why don't you plan to have Maria here around eight?"

"Will do. See you then, sis." He planted a kiss on her cheek, grabbed her plate of uneaten eggs and dug in.

"Your car or mine?" Wayne held the door open for Piper and she walked out into the early morning quiet.

"Doesn't matter to me." But once they decided, she needed to ask him if he'd looked for the paperwork regarding the antiques she was missing. The thought sat like lead in her belly, and she was glad she'd skipped the eggs.

"Then we'll take mine. I don't trust that old clunker of yours."

"Clunker? I'll have you know that's a vintage 1968 GTO. There are men who would fall to their knees and beg for my hand in marriage just for the chance to drive it."

"Yeah, well, I'll take reliable over vintage beauty any day."

"I have to agree, reliable can be nice. The GTO's been in the shop twice this month." Piper leaned her head back against the leather headrest of Wayne's sedan. "New has a lot of advantages."

"It's also expensive."

There was a tone to Wayne's voice that Piper hadn't heard before. She shifted in her seat, trying to see his expression in the dim morning light, all thoughts of cars and missing antiques gone. "Is everything okay, Wayne?"

"Sure. Everything is fine."

"I've known you long enough to know when you're not telling the truth. So spill. What's up?"

"Nothing serious. Just a lot of bills to pay. Marcus's funeral was expensive. Plus, we've had a lot of medical bills the past few years."

"I thought Marcus had health insurance."

"He did, but some things weren't covered. He had some experimental treatments done. We flew to Mexico three different times trying to find something that would slow the progress of the disease."

"Marcus said you were vacationing."

"Because he didn't want anyone to try and talk him out of it." He paused, shrugged. "It was expensive. Then there was the broken hip, the pneumonia, medication, deductibles. It added up."

The burden must have been compounded when Marcus stepped down from his job as CEO of Music Makers and gave up teaching piano lessons in the months prior to his death. Wayne didn't say as much, though Piper was sure he was thinking it. "Why didn't you say something, Wayne? My family and I would have helped."

"I owed this to Marcus. He gave me a second chance, Piper. He believed in me enough to help me start over. I wanted him to live the last years of his life with dignity, not begging for money from his family. Besides, I thought when the time came and he passed on, I'd use his life insurance money to pay any debt we accrued."

"Can't you?"

"Not if the insurance company won't pay."

"But they have to."

Wayne didn't respond, just accelerated onto the highway, his lips set in a hard line, his jaw tight.

"What aren't you telling me?"

"Let's drop the subject."

"Let's not."

"You want to know the truth? The insurance company says Marcus's death was suspicious."

"What? Why? Marcus didn't have an enemy in the world."

"Yeah. He did. Himself. Come on, Piper, don't you get it? He was a musician, a teacher, a performer. Imagine if your body started failing you. Imagine if all the things you loved most were things you could no longer do."

"You don't mean they think he committed suicide?"

"That's exactly what I mean."

"That's ridiculous. Marcus would never—"

"Wouldn't he?"

"Of course not."

They were both silent, the tension in the car thick and filled with unspoken thoughts. Finally, Piper put a hand on Wayne's shoulder. "He didn't commit suicide. Marcus wasn't a quitter. Ever."

"One way or another, I can't fight this. If I hire a lawyer, the insurance company's suspicions will go public. Imagine what that will mean for Music Makers."

"And what will it mean for you if you don't?"

"Let's just say the picture isn't a pretty one."

"So let's tell my parents and my brothers. Between the seven of us, we can pay whatever you owe."

"No. Marcus told me over and over again that he didn't want to be a burden to his family. I plan to honor that wish, no matter what it takes."

"How could you think that Marcus would want to leave this all on your shoulders?"

"Marcus bailed me out of a ten-thousand-dollar debt. If he hadn't, I would have gone to jail. Did you know that?"

She hadn't, and wondered why not. She'd known Wayne for years, and it seemed she didn't know him at all. "No. I didn't."

"Now you do. I was young and stupid and took money that didn't belong to me. I called it borrowing, but the real term is embezzlement. I used it to gamble. And lost every penny of it. Wayne bailed me out. Because of him, I got community service and restitution instead of jail. Paying off his debt is my way of paying him back."

"Wayne—"

"Let it go, Piper."

She didn't want to. She wanted to ask a million questions. Questions she should have asked long ago, and might have if her life hadn't been so cluttered, so filled with work and obligations. She glanced at

Wayne—his firm jaw, dark brown hair and wire-rimmed glasses so familiar to her. How was it that she could know so little about him? "Wayne, I really—"

"How about some music?" He cut her off purposely, almost rudely, and Piper knew he was finished with the conversation, whether she liked it or not.

She sighed, rubbed the bridge of her nose, trying to rid herself of the headache that threatened. "Classical?"

"Contemporary."

"Christian?"

"Country."

"Tell me you're joking."

"Hey, aren't you the one who says there's value in every kind of music?" He smirked, switched on the radio and started singing along.

Deborah James looked exactly like her voice had sounded over the phone—sweet, pretty and feminine. Shoulder-length brown hair highlighted to golden blond, blue eyes wide and thickly lashed, she spoke with a soft airy voice that belied the strength in her handshake and in her gaze. "Thank you for coming."

"It's our pleasure." Wayne spoke before Piper could, moving into the house behind Deborah, his gaze taking in the room and the woman.

"I should have mailed everything to you, but I wasn't sure if you'd need it all, and going through everything just seemed…"

"Please, don't worry about it. Wayne and I were happy to come and look through the files."

"My husband was very organized, so it shouldn't take long."

"Were you married long?"

"Five years. Not nearly long enough."

"I can only imagine how devastating this is for you."

"It has been hard." Deborah smoothed a hand over thick straight hair and met Piper's gaze. "The senselessness of the accident makes it even worse. To have the person you love alive and whole one minute, and lying broken on the pavement the next..." She swallowed back tears. "Jason was crossing at a crosswalk. He should have been safe."

"Was the driver charged?" Wayne asked the question as Deborah opened a file cabinet and pulled out two thick file folders.

"No. It was a hit-and-run accident. They never found the driver."

"I'm so sorry." If Piper had known Deborah, she might have hugged her. Instead, she patted a hand against the other woman's shoulder.

"Me, too. Here are the files. I did try to go through and see what might be useful, but as I said, it was too overwhelming. You're welcome to look through it here and leave anything you don't want. I've also got a box of photos and tapes that are marked Music Makers."

Piper took the folders, the weight of the pages inside surprising her. "Your husband did a lot of research."

"He wanted the story to be special. Marcus was somewhat of a hero to him. Jason attended a Music

Makers summer camp when he was a kid. He always said it changed his life. Gave him something to focus on besides getting in trouble. He's been playing guitar ever since." She grabbed a box from the floor, held it out to Wayne.

If she realized she'd spoken in the present tense, Deborah's expression didn't reveal it.

She leaned over, pulled another file from the cabinet. "I almost forgot this one. It's information my husband received from Marcus. Names and things. Do you want to take it, as well?"

"Sure, I—"

"Didn't John give you names and contact information already?" Wayne had stepped up beside Piper and was eyeing the heavy folders.

"Yes, but I'll take this anyway. There might be notes from Marcus interspersed with the information."

Wayne shrugged. "Your choice."

Piper put the folders into her briefcase, knowing she'd have to go through them and not sure when she'd find the time. Maybe tomorrow after church. If not then, Monday before piano lessons. "Thank you so much, Mrs. James. I'll send you a copy of the book when it's finished."

"I'd like that. And I know Jason would be happy knowing his notes and interviews were being put to good use." She blinked back tears. "Listen, would you like to stay for a cup of coffee? I should have offered before, but—"

"Oh, no. Please, don't worry about it. We're fine."

"Are you sure? I'm not being a very good hostess."

"You don't need to be. You need to take care of yourself right now. Not other people." Wayne sounded so unlike himself that Piper cast a quick look in his direction. He watched Deborah with a mixture of admiration and interest so obvious Piper wanted to elbow him in the ribs.

She chose the next best thing. "We have to head home. If you have any questions about the book, or just want to see how it's progressing, give me a call."

"That's kind of you."

"Thanks again." Piper nudged Wayne out the door, trying not to smile as he slid into the car.

He still looked tired, but there was a new energy to him. An energy Piper had seen enough of in her brothers to recognize. "That went well."

He glanced at Piper as he pulled out of Deborah's driveway. "I guess so."

"Deborah seems nice."

"It's hard to tell during a five-minute conversation."

"You think so?"

"Sure do. First impressions are overrated. Too many people have perfected the art of subterfuge."

"That's a cynical thing to say, Wayne."

"Might be, but it's still true."

Surprised, Piper tried to read Wayne's expression. She could see nothing but what she'd always seen— a quietly attractive man with a sometimes too-serious expression. "And you know this because?"

"I lived an entire life before I came to Lakeview,

Piper. Just because I don't talk about it, doesn't mean it isn't there."

"What—"

"And the reason I haven't talked about it is because I haven't wanted to. So, how about we change the subject?"

For a moment Piper could think of nothing to say. Her mind scrambled with bits and pieces of information she'd learned over the years. There hadn't been much. Some talk about Wayne's father being in jail. A mention of his murder by a fellow inmate. Piper hadn't spent much time thinking about it. Now she wondered if she should have asked, shown some interest in the life Wayne lived before his mother married Marcus. "What—"

"Don't." Wayne's voice was sharp, the look he shot at Piper hot and angry.

"Don't what?"

"Don't ask questions. I won't answer them. The past is what it is. I try hard to live in the here and now."

Piper tapped her fingers against her knees and waited for Wayne to fill the silence. When he didn't, she reached for the radio. "How about some music?"

He glanced her way, gave her a half smile. "Contemporary?"

"Classical."

"Go for it."

SEVEN

It was just past two when Wayne pulled his car back into Piper's driveway. The tension between them had disappeared hours ago, and Piper smiled as she pushed open the door. "Thanks for coming with me, Wayne."

"It wasn't a problem."

"Listen, I hate to be a nag, but have you had a chance to look through Marcus's records? I'm trying to complete the inventory and get everything to the appraiser. The three items I mentioned to you are the only ones on the list the lawyer gave me that I can't account for."

He hesitated, then shook his head. "Not yet, but we could go to Music Makers and look through Marcus's files there. If we don't find anything, I'll check his home office this evening."

That wasn't what Piper wanted to hear. What she wanted to hear was that he'd take care of it, that he'd do what he'd already said he would and search for the information himself.

She couldn't say that, so she did what she always did and agreed. "When do you want to do it?"

"Now is as good as any time. Unless you've got plans?"

She did have plans, but finding the antiques was just as important. If she couldn't locate records of their sale, she'd have to assume they'd been stolen. That would mean contacting the police, filling out reports...

"Piper? You still with me?" Wayne's voice broke into her thoughts, and she nodded.

"Sorry, I was just thinking about what I need to get done today."

"Like I said, if you have plans—"

"Nothing that can't wait a few hours."

"I'll call John, then. See if he minds opening up the building."

Five minutes later, Piper was in her GTO, singing along with a tape of traditional worship songs as she followed Wayne to Music Makers' corporate office in Lynchburg's historic district. Housed in a four-story brick building, the foundation was as much a part of Piper's life as playing piano and teaching. As a child she'd spent hours there, listening to her uncle and his business partner, John Sweeny, discuss scholarships, school grants and summer camp programs. Even then, she'd been impressed by her uncle's passion for providing music education to underprivileged kids, but it wasn't until she was an adult that she understood how much energy and time Marcus had put into making his dream a reality.

She pulled into the parking lot behind the building and parked next to Wayne's sedan. He'd already gone inside, and she hurried after him, her eyes scanning the bushes that dotted the perimeter of the blacktop. A hush hung over the area, insects and birds silent, even the sound of traffic muted, as if the world were holding its breath and waiting.

Piper shuddered, shoving open the door and stepping inside. Marcus's office had been on the third floor, and Piper headed there, the odd feeling she'd had in the parking lot following her up flight after flight of stairs. Maybe it was the empty offices, the silent halls, the darkened doorways. Whatever the case, Piper's heart pumped with a fear that made no sense, but that couldn't be ignored.

A light shone at the end of the third floor hall, and Piper hurried toward it, relieved when she saw Wayne and John Sweeny sitting at a desk in Marcus's old office.

Co-founder of Music Makers and current CEO of the company, John had the courtly manners of another era, and stood as Piper entered the room, his hands reaching for hers and offering a gentle squeeze. "How are you, my dear?"

"I'm good, Mr. Sweeny."

"I'm glad to hear it. I was worried when I saw you on the news the other night, but it seems you're no worse for wear."

"I'm not. How about you? Is everything going well?"

"Fine, fine. Though nothing has been the same since Marcus passed away. His passion for music and for this company can't be replaced." He raked a hand through thick gray hair and smiled, his blue-green eyes sad.

"I know, but having you here in his place is exactly what he wanted."

"What Marcus wanted was to live long enough to see every child given the gift of a music education. I'm afraid I don't have his faith that that will happen in my lifetime, but perhaps if we keep his dream alive long enough… I'm getting maudlin. You're here to look for some missing antiques?"

"Actually, we're looking for anything that could prove Marcus sold the items."

"This is a good place to start, then. Marcus did sell a few items over the years, and put the money into Music Makers' coffers. Though I can't say I remember any recent sales. What are you missing?"

"A jeweled coronet. A Beatles album signed by all of the Beatles. A handwritten music score by Gershwin."

"No. I definitely don't remember those things being sold, but you never know until you check. We've kept Marcus's office intact for now. Too painful to come in and clean it out. Take a look through the file cabinets. If you need any of the archived files, you'll find them in the basement."

"Thank you, Mr. Sweeny. Ready to get started, Wayne? I've got to be back in Lakeview in a few hours."

"Sure. Let's do it."

"I won't keep you." John smiled and stepped toward the door. "Let me know if there's anything else I can do for you, Piper. Either in searching for these items, or in researching for the book."

"I appreciate it. You've already helped tremendously."

"I've got a vested interest. If things go as planned, the book will be a phenomenal promotional tool for the foundation."

"Then let's hope it goes as planned."

"With you writing it, the book can be no less than wonderful. Did you make your trip to Richmond, yet?"

"I did. Thank Jessie for me. I'm glad she thought to give Mrs. James my number."

"And was the information helpful in your research?"

Piper laughed. "I'll tell you as soon as I have a minute to look at it."

He gave her a slight smile, issued a curt nod in Wayne's direction. "You'll lock up?"

"Of course."

"Then I'll leave you to your search."

Wayne pulled open the first file cabinet as John stepped out of the room. "None of these look like personal files, but that doesn't mean there aren't any here. How do you want to search?"

"You take the first cabinet. I'll do the second. Then we'll check the desk."

"Sounds good. Let's get to it."

* * *

Two hours later they'd worked their way through the office file cabinets. "Nothing." Piper shut the last file drawer and sighed with frustration.

"I'll check at home tonight and get back to you."

How many times in the past weeks had he said that? Too many.

If Piper had the time she'd insist on going home with Wayne, insist on helping with the search. She didn't. She was already running behind today, so she bit her lip and kept silent.

Obviously, Wayne had a lot on his mind. If he didn't give her a call by Monday, she'd have to call him and give him a gentle nudge in the right direction.

Evening shadows stretched across the blacktop as Piper stepped outside. She'd have to hurry if she were going to get to the store *and* stop by Cade's house. A picture of the inside of her refrigerator flashed through her mind. No milk. No eggs. No bread. One soda. She glanced at the dashboard clock and grimaced. Maybe she'd stop at Cade's house first, then go to the store. That way she wouldn't have to leave perishable items sitting in the car.

She was ten minutes from home when the GTO shimmied to the left, the soft thump and bump of a flat tire unmistakable. "Perfect."

She sighed, pulled to the shoulder and got out to survey the damage. "Flat as a pancake."

Good thing she knew how to change a tire. She popped open the trunk and pulled out the tire iron and carjack. It wouldn't take long to fix the problem, but even a small amount of time seemed like a big deal when she had so much to do. "I guess you're trying to teach me something, Lord."

What it was, she didn't know. Maybe when she had time, she'd sit down and figure it out. For now, she needed to concentrate on the work at hand, get it done, and move on to the next task.

She'd barely begun when the sound of a car engine filled the air. A dark sedan sped into view, slowing as it neared Piper. She peered into the evening gloom, trying to make out the driver, but could see nothing but a metal pole that stuck out the window and glinted in the fading light. No, wait, not a pole. A gun!

Piper threw herself sideways as the sound of a gunshot cracked through the air. Burning pain sliced across her shoulder, but she didn't have time to think about it. The car picked up speed, braked hard and spun in a U-turn.

From her position beside the GTO, Piper could see it all, knew that in seconds the car would be back, the gun at the ready again. She belly-crawled to her car door, praying she could get it open, grab her cell phone and call for help. Of course, by the time help arrived she'd probably be dead.

Maybe running was the better option. Heart in her throat, she levered up, looking for the chance she needed. Another shot rang out, and Piper flinched as dirt and debris exploded a few yards from her position. Where were all the cars, all the people that should be coming back from Lynchburg at this time of evening?

As if her thoughts had conjured it, the sound of another engine sounded above the pounding of Piper's pulse. Tires squealed and the sedan sped out of sight.

Piper tried to stand, wanting to wave down the truck that was approaching, but her legs didn't want to hold her. She grabbed the side of the car to pull herself up, her hand slipping against smooth metal, a trail of bright red blood smearing the sky-blue paint.

"Come on, Dad, you can't sit here moping for the rest of your life."

"Watch me." Sean Macalister folded his good arm across his chest, and speared Cade with a look that shouted "go ahead, try to make me do it."

"I don't want to get in another argument about this."

"Then don't."

"Fine. Then I'll just tell you how it's going to be. I've invited a friend over. When she gets here, you're not going to hide in this room. You're going to say hello, make conversation. Do what any normal person would do."

"There's one problem with that, son." Sean waved his left hand in the air, gestured to the wheelchair he was sitting in. "I'm not normal."

"You're right, you're not normal. You're ornery. But Dr. Jennings still wants you to push yourself more. You can't improve if—"

"Save it. I've heard the lecture. There's no need for a repeat."

Cade gritted his teeth to keep from saying something he shouldn't. Things had been tough before they'd moved back to Lakeview, Sean's independent spirit challenged by partial paralysis and muscle weakness. Now, things were ten times worse. Unfortunately, arguing, lecturing and pushing his father had done no good, and right now, Cade was too frustrated to keep trying. "Have it your way, Dad. I'll leave you to yourself."

He stepped out of his father's room, muscles tight with tension, jaw clamped around the words that wanted to spill out. He grabbed a bottle of water from the avocado-green refrigerator, flipped on the CB scanner and settled into a chair. Piper should be calling soon. Maybe when she arrived, his dad would change his mind. If not, Cade would have to come up with another plan to draw Sean out of his self-imposed prison.

"Someone's been shot?"

"What?" Cade turned, saw his father sitting at the doorway to the kitchen.

"You've got that CB blasting loud enough to wake the dead, and you can't hear what it's saying?"

"I've had other things on my mind."

"Well, get them out of your mind and listen, 'cause to me it sounds like someone's been shot out on Old Dairy Farm Road."

Cade turned his attention to the tinny voices, the

excitement and anxiety of the speakers obvious. His dad was right. There had been a shooting.

Cade adjusted the scanner, tried to find out more.

"You going to sit there listening all night, or go over there and see what's what?"

"I'm not on duty." Though Cade was itching to get in his car and drive to the scene.

"That ever stopped you before?"

He shrugged, ignoring the question.

"When's your friend coming?"

"She'll call when she's on the way."

"And she hasn't called yet. So, let's go. It's what? A ten-minute drive? Your friend doesn't reach you here she'll call your cell phone. Meantime, we can get a look at the action."

"We?"

"You wanted to get me out of the house. Here's your chance. Let's go see what's happening."

"Dad, that's—"

"What? Not a good idea? Too dangerous? Come on, son, I'm fifty-eight. Old enough to stay out of your hair and out of trouble, chair or no chair."

"That isn't the point."

"Then what is?"

"That we don't want to clutter up a crime scene. That there will be ambulances, police cars and dozens of people doing jobs that shouldn't be interfered with."

"Who said anything about interfering?"

Cade's cell phone rang, cutting off his reply. He

glanced at the caller ID, saw Jake Reed's number and picked up. "Macalister, here."

"You doing anything right now?"

"Listening to my scanner. Sounds like you've got trouble."

"We do. I wouldn't mind having a photographer working on this one. We've got skid marks and some clear tread marks."

"I'll be there in ten." He grabbed his camera, glanced at Sean. "If you really want to go, let's head out."

"I only said what I did because I didn't think you'd even consider it."

"You were wrong."

Sean eyed him for a moment, and then shrugged. "Let's go, then."

Police and ambulance sirens blared in the distance as Cade drove toward the north side of town and turned onto Old Dairy Farm Road. Lined with trees, it curved around the lake and wound its way to Lynchburg. Not the most popular route between the two towns, it was still well used. That a shooting had occurred there seemed inconceivable.

"Road rage," Sean said as two police cruisers and an ambulance came into view.

"What's that, Dad?"

"Must have been some out of control driver, taking out his frustration with a gun. It happens all the time. Saw a whole program on it yesterday."

"I think you've been watching too many talk shows." Cade pulled in behind one of the cruisers and parked his car. "Stay here. I'm going to check things out."

"Like I'd be going anywhere. The chair's in the trunk, remember?"

Cade didn't bother to respond, just closed the door on his father's scowling glare and walked toward the crime scene.

He noticed the car first—sky-blue, polished to a deep shine, it was a one-of-a-kind GTO. Piper's car. His gut clenched with the knowledge, and he strode toward it, ignoring the crime-scene tape and angry shout of a uniformed officer he didn't recognize.

"I said stop! This is a crime scene." Six-four, hazel eyes in a dark tan face, the officer moved toward Cade with fluid, pantherlike movements that spoke of training in the martial arts. He'd be a worthy opponent on the mat, but this wasn't a sparring match and Cade had no intention of making it into one.

He forced himself to relax. "I'm a police officer. Cade Macalister." He pulled out his wallet and flashed the badge he carried.

"Macalister? The sheriff is expecting you. He's in the ambulance with the victim. Watch your head if you go in there. The lady is fighting mad. Thinks we should let her drive home."

If he weren't so worried, Cade would have smiled at that. "She badly hurt?"

"Hard to tell. It's a shoulder wound. Could be serious, but she seemed well enough when we got here."

Which meant nothing when it came to gunshot wounds. Cade had seen too many victims who'd been lucid one minute and dead the next.

The back of the ambulance was open, the area beyond filled to overflowing with two EMTs and the sheriff. "Sheriff?"

Jake turned, his eyes flashing, his expression grim. "Macalister. Thanks for coming."

"No problem." He stepped up into the ambulance and caught sight of Piper.

Face leeched of color, the bandage that covered her shoulder stained with blood, she still managed a smile. "It doesn't look like I'm going to be stopping by your house tonight."

"Another night, then. Looks like you took a hit."

"Nothing life threatening. They're taking me to the hospital anyway. *And* poking me full of holes." She shot a look at the EMT, who stood beside her hanging an IV bag.

He didn't even glance her way, just finished what he was doing as he spoke. "One hole. The guy with the gun did a lot more damage and you're not complaining about him. Are we ready to head out, sheriff?"

Jake gave a curt nod. "I'll see you at the hospital, Piper. I've already called Grayson. He should be there by the time you arrive."

"Thanks." She looked scared, vulnerable, so unlike herself that Cade wanted to take her in his arms and tell her everything was going to be okay.

Somehow he doubted she'd appreciate the sentiment.

"Come on, Macalister. Let's get those photos."

Cade left reluctantly, following Jake out into the street, and eyeing the skid marks that blackened the pavement and led into the dirt at the side of the road. "Looks like our guy did a U-turn. Then swerved off the road."

"That's what Piper said. And our witness." Jake gestured to a teal pickup truck parked at the side of the road. "Unfortunately, neither got a license plate number or a description of the driver."

"So we've got nothing." Cade raised his camera and took a close-up shot of the skid mark.

"Nothing but a flat tire that might have been tampered with and some tread marks."

"You've got evidence?" Cade moved to the side of the road, snapped pictures of the tread marks.

"Take a look at the nail we pulled out of the tire." Jake took an evidence bag from his pocket, used tweezers to pull out a shiny silver nail.

"It's new."

"Makes you wonder, doesn't it?"

"Where was she this afternoon? Who was she with?"

"Music Makers' headquarters in Lynchburg. Wayne was with her."

"Marcus's stepson. Does he have anything to gain from her death?"

"Close to a million dollars' worth of antiques. A house worth another couple hundred thousand."

"In other words, he'll gain plenty." Cade took a couple of shots of the tire. "Anyone else with her?"

"The CEO of Music Makers. Can't find a motive for him, but that doesn't mean much. That your father?" He gestured toward Cade's car.

Sean had managed to get out, and was leaning against the door, a look of stubborn determination on his face.

"Yes, that's him."

"I guess you finally got him out of the house."

"And up on his feet."

"Even better. Let's finish up. Then one of us needs to go to the hospital, see if Piper has remembered anything else. The sooner we get the guy who did this, the better I'll feel."

Two hours later, Cade wheeled Sean in through the emergency room entrance of the hospital and parked his wheelchair in the lobby. "Are you sure you'll be okay here for a few minutes?"

"I said I wanted to come, didn't I?" Obviously, getting out of the house hadn't improved Sean's disposition.

"Do you have money for coffee or a soda?"

"I'm not a kid, Cade. Go visit your lady and leave me be."

Cade bit back a sharp retort, forcing himself to be civil, despite his irritation. "See you in a few, Dad."

The admissions nurse glanced up as Cade flashed his badge, shrugged a slim shoulder and gestured him through the double doors that led to the treatment area. "Triage room five. She's already got too many people in there with her, but go ahead through anyway."

Cade found the room easily, the sound of voices carrying through the closed door. He knocked, waited until someone called for him to enter and pushed the door open.

"Come in. If you can find a spot that isn't already filled." The frustration in Piper's voice was obvious, though the rest of the people in the room didn't seem to notice.

Cade counted five—Grayson, a petite, dark-haired woman, a man with shaggy blond hair, another with dark brown hair and wire-rimmed glasses and a nurse who hovered over Piper, her hands fiddling with the IV line, her eyes darting from one person to another.

Definitely a crowd. And if Cade were reading things correctly, it was a crowd Piper would be happier without. "I hate to break up the party, but I'm with the Lakeview Sheriff's Department. I've got some questions I need to ask Piper. I'll have to ask you all to step outside."

The man with the wire-rimmed glasses nodded, bent to kiss Piper's cheek. "Call me if you need anything."

"Thanks, Wayne."

Wayne. The man who stood to gain so much from Piper's death. He seemed solicitous enough as he said goodbye to Piper, brushed a strand of hair from her forehead and left. Was it possible he'd punctured Piper's tire, followed her and shot her?

Maybe. Eventually, Cade would find the truth. Until then, he'd keep a careful eye on Piper and on the people in her life.

"Any news on who did this?" Grayson cut into Cade's speculation.

"We've put out an APB on the gunman's vehicle, but chances are we won't find it. The description we've got is too vague. We've got no license plate number. No description of the driver."

"So what do you have?" The question was quiet and low, the man who spoke it so still he almost faded into the background. Almost. His height and weight were average. His mid-blond hair cut in a non-descript style. His clothes unremarkable. It was his eyes that made him stand out. Not the odd gray of Piper and Grayson's, but an intense, deep blue that Cade recognized immediately.

"Tristan. It's been a while."

"Sixteen years." He eyed Cade for a moment, his gaze assessing. "I'd say it was nice to see you again, but the circumstances don't warrant it. Do you have anything besides vague descriptions to go on? Or are you flying blind on this one?"

"We've got tread marks and a bullet. Neither will do any good unless we can find the car and gun they came from."

Tristan nodded, stepped toward his sister. "I'd better get out of here. I've got a flight to catch in a few hours. Be careful, kid. I'd hate to get called home from Egypt because something happened to you." He leaned forward to drop a kiss on her forehead.

"You be careful, too. I'd hate to be called *to* Egypt because something happened to *you*."

"No worries. I'm in more danger of being talked to death by my students than I am of getting hurt."

"Be careful, anyway."

"Will do. See you when I get home." He squeezed her hand, clapped Grayson on the back and walked out of the room.

Two down. Three more to go. And Cade had a feeling Grayson would be a lot more difficult to remove from the room.

Fortunately, it seemed the woman beside him was tired of being at the hospital.

She sighed, ran her hand up Grayson's bicep, brushing an imaginary piece of lint off his shoulder. "Darling, we really do need to get going. I've got an eight o'clock phone conference and it won't do for me to miss it. Piper will be fine here with Officer… I'm sorry, I didn't catch your name."

"Macalister. Cade."

"I'm Maria Jessup, Grayson's fiancée. You will take good care of our Piper, won't you? I really do need to get home."

"I don't think—" Grayson started to protest, but Piper cut him short.

"I'll be fine, Gray."

He hesitated, then shrugged. "All right. Call me when you're ready to go home. I'll pick you up."

He took Maria's arm and led her out the door.

Which left the nurse.

Cade turned his attention to her, watching as she checked the IV again. "Has the doctor been in yet?"

She glanced up, met his eyes. "Yes. We're waiting on X-ray results."

"Maybe you could go check, see if they're ready?"

"Of course. I'll be back shortly." She left the room, back ramrod straight, a frown drawing down the corners of her mouth.

Bingo!

EIGHT

The door closed with a quiet thud, and Piper swallowed back a shout of joy. After hours of people hovering over her, asking questions, checking and double-checking to see if she was all right, she was finally alone.

Well, almost alone.

"So how'd I do?" Cade pulled a chair over and sat down beside her, a half smile easing the tension from his face.

"Do?"

"At clearing the room."

"Was I that obvious?"

"Let's just say you looked less than pleased."

"I was, but not just because everyone was hovering over me."

"No? What's upsetting you?"

"Besides the fact that someone tried to kill me?"

"Besides that."

"Nothing."

"So, let's talk about what happened. Jake said you didn't see the gunman."

"No. I was too busy diving for cover to get a good look."

"You saw the car, though."

"It was a dark sedan. A lot like Wayne's."

His eyes narrowed, and Piper cut him off before he could say what she knew he was thinking. "It wasn't Wayne."

"You're sure of that?"

"Of course I am."

Cade eyed her for a moment, his gaze taking in every detail of her appearance. "Sometimes we want to believe in someone who doesn't deserve our trust."

"This isn't one of those times."

He looked like he wanted to argue, but let the subject drop instead. "Can you think of anyone else who'd want to hurt you?"

"No."

"Co-workers? Ex-boyfriends? Anyone who may be holding a grudge?"

"My life just isn't that exciting." At least it hadn't been, until recently.

"You're working on a book about Music Makers?"

"Yes, but I don't see—"

"And getting ready for its twenty-fifth anniversary celebration?"

"Yes."

"Has anything come up during your research,

anything that you questioned, anything that didn't make sense?"

"Nothing." Except for the missing antiques. They didn't make sense. The fact that she couldn't find records of sales didn't make sense.

"You're quiet. Did you think of something?"

Should she tell him? If she did, would the information point toward Wayne?

"Piper, someone wants you dead. If you know something, now would be the time to tell me." He leaned close, staring into her eyes as if he could see the truth there.

"It's nothing. Not really. I inherited a collection of musical antiquities from my uncle. His lawyer gave me an inventory of the items Marcus named in his will. I haven't been able to locate three of them."

"Have you reported this to the police?"

"There hasn't been a need yet. There's still a possibility the items will be accounted for. Wayne thinks they were sold. We're searching for sales records now. That's why we were at Music Makers this evening."

"Wayne again. I think I'm seeing a pattern here."

"You don't think he stole the antiques from my uncle?"

"I don't know, but I plan to find out."

"Look, Wayne is family—"

"And family is capable of unspeakable atrocities."

"I know, but—" The door opened before she could say more in Wayne's defense and Dr. Brian McMath strode in.

A chart in his hand, a scowl on his face, he looked irritated and didn't seem afraid to show it. "I hear you're getting impatient."

Piper eased into a sitting position, wincing a little as the stitches Brian had put in her shoulder stretched and pulled. "Not at all. I enjoy sitting in an emergency room for hours at a time."

"No need for sarcasm, Piper."

"I'm not being sarcastic. I'm being facetious."

"I'd say the two are the same. Let me take a look at that knee again." He flipped up the sheet that covered her legs, poked at the swollen, bruised flesh of her left knee.

Her skin went cold and clammy, her stomach heaving with the pain. "Ow!"

"The X-ray is clean. No break."

"There will be soon if you don't stop poking at it like that, Doc." Cade's tone and expression were sharp, his gaze hard.

"I'm doing my job, Mr.—?"

"Cade Macalister. I'm with the sheriff's department."

"I see. And I'm sure Piper appreciates your efforts on her behalf, but it might be best if you wait outside." Arrogance seeped through every word, just as it had when Piper had gone out to dinner with him a few months ago.

One of the reasons she'd not repeated the experience.

"I don't think so." Cade crossed his arms over his

chest and leaned back in the chair. "You said the knee wasn't broken. Obviously something *is* wrong with it."

"A few wrenched ligaments. Nothing that won't heal on its own." Brian turned his back on Cade, prodding the knee again. "I'll wrap it. Give you a crutch to use. You'll be good as new in no time."

"How long?"

"Ten days. Two weeks." He shrugged. "We'll check it again when you come in to get your stitches out. You can make an appointment with my office. Come in around lunchtime and we can get a bite to eat afterward."

Piper gritted her teeth to keep from telling him what he could do with his bite to eat. "Thanks. I'll probably see my general practitioner, though."

Cade watched the interplay between Piper and the doctor with interest. Obviously, they were acquaintances. It didn't seem that Piper wanted more than that. The doctor was another story. In the time it took for him to wrap her knee, McMath managed to ask Piper out two more times.

She deftly sidestepped the invitations, and McMath grew more frustrated by the minute, his face clouding, his gestures becoming more abrupt. Apparently the doctor didn't want to take no for an answer.

"That's done." McMath straightened, looked at the IV bag. "IV antibiotics are almost finished, too. I'll write a prescription for painkillers. I'm off in twenty minutes if you want a ride home."

"My brother is going to pick me up."

"He'll probably be happy not to have to come back to the hospital. Give him a ring. Let him know I've got it covered."

"I appreciate the offer, Brian, but Grayson is going to drive me home." Piper's cheerful good humor had frayed around the edges, fatigue and pain painting fine lines around her eyes and mouth.

"Like I said, that isn't necessary. I can—"

"You can get the prescription and Piper's discharge orders and let her be on her way," Cade suggested.

"I don't think this is any of your business, Officer Macalister." Obviously, McMath didn't know when to give up.

"What you think doesn't matter. What matters is that your patient has told you twice that she doesn't need or want any extra attention. She's got a ride home, and her own general practitioner will do follow-up. I'm not sure what part of that you didn't understand."

"I understood perfectly. I'm just not sure Piper is thinking straight."

"She's not the one having trouble thinking straight."

McMath's lips tightened into a thin line, his boy-next-door good looks marred by anger.

Cade thought for sure he'd continue the argument. Instead he turned abruptly. "I'll send the nurse in with the paperwork and prescription."

The door slammed behind his retreating figure, and Piper breathed a sigh of relief. "I don't know what he was thinking. I've never seen Brian act that way before."

"You know him well?"

"Not really. We met when I started attending Grace Christian Church. About three months ago. He asked me to lunch after the service."

"And you agreed to go with him?"

"Yes." Much to her regret.

"And that was your only date?"

"I don't consider lunch after church a date."

"*He* does."

"I'm not sure I understand what you're getting at." But she was beginning to, her mind scrambling back over the past few months, cataloguing the times she'd run into Brian in the hall at church, at the store, how many times he'd called her, asked her to dinner or out to lunch. "No way."

"What?" Cade studied her with an intensity that made her want to look away.

"There's no way Brian has anything to do with the shooting."

"Maybe not."

"Look, he's arrogant and hardheaded, but he's not a stalker."

"Like I said, maybe not, but I wouldn't be very good at my job if I closed my mind to the possibility. Does McMath have your phone number? Does he know where you live?"

"Yes to the first. Probably to the second."

"And he calls you?"

"Once or twice a week."

"To ask you out."

It wasn't a question, but Piper answered anyway. "Usually."

"So you've been turning him down for months."

"Nicely, but, yeah, I've been turning him down."

"I think we'll take a closer look at Dr. McMath. See if anything turns up."

"Is that really necessary? What if it gets out that you're investigating him? It might hurt his career."

"He's got nothing to worry about unless he's hiding something."

"I still don't like the idea."

"That's because you're too nice." He smiled, the dimple in his cheek flashing, and Piper's heart did a little flip.

She turned away, picking at the frayed edge of the jeans that had been cut off at the thigh when she'd arrived. "I'm a pushover, you mean."

"You're no pushover."

"No?"

"No. A pushover is someone who is too weak to fight for what she wants, or what she knows is right. You're definitely not that." He brushed a few strands of hair away from her cheek, his hand lingering, his fingers grazing the tender flesh behind her ear.

"Okay. So I'm not a pushover. I'm just too nice. I'm not sure I like that any better."

Cade laughed and stood. "Hey, there's nothing wrong with being nice. Now, how about I go find my father and we give you a ride home?"

"Your father is here?"

"Yes. You didn't even have to ask him to dog-sit to pull him out of his shell."

"All it took was a bullet to my shoulder."

"We'll have to think of something less drastic to get him to agree to the next meeting. I'll be back in a minute."

"Are you sure? I wouldn't want to put you out." And she wasn't sure spending more time with Cade was a good idea.

"You won't be."

Piper was silent for a moment and Cade knew she was thinking through the pros and cons of his offer. Finally, she met his gaze. "Would you mind stopping by my car? I left my purse and briefcase there."

"I grabbed them both from the scene. They're in my car."

"Why am I not surprised?"

"Because you've seen how organized and efficient I am?"

"More like, I've seen how much like my brothers you are."

"And that's a bad thing?"

"Not really. My brothers are great guys."

"But they drive you crazy?"

"Something like that." She smiled, eased to her feet, apparently ready to end the conversation. "Thanks for getting my stuff. It's one less thing I need to worry about."

"No problem." A knock sounded at the door

before Cade could say more, and the nurse stepped into the room.

"Dr. McMath asked me to go over a few things with you before you leave, Ms. Sinclair."

"I'll meet you back here in a few minutes." Cade moved toward the door, reluctant to leave.

"Let's meet in the lobby instead. The sooner I get out of this room, the better."

"Sounds good."

Piper watched Cade leave and wished she were going with him. She told herself it was because she was tired of sitting like a prisoner in the triage room. The truth was, having Cade around was comforting. Maybe too comforting. Unlike her brothers and Wayne, Cade hadn't expected constant reassurance that she was okay. He hadn't seemed to expect anything at all.

And that was something she wasn't used to.

"If you'll have a seat, Ms. Sinclair, I'll take out your IV and get you on your way." The nurse sounded as impatient and harried as Piper felt, and Piper lowered herself back onto the gurney trying to smile past her pain and fatigue.

"Thanks."

A few minutes later she was free, hobbling through the corridor and toward escape.

"You should be in a wheelchair." Brian McMath's voice cut through the hum of hospital activity.

"I'm fine." Piper would have hobbled faster if it had been possible on one crutch.

Unfortunately, it wasn't, and Brian stepped up

beside her, matching pace for pace. "You've got twenty stitches in your shoulder and a strained knee. Let me get—"

"Brian, I said I'm fine." The sharpness in her voice didn't seem to faze him. Instead of backing off and letting her alone, he followed her into the lobby.

"Stay here. I'll go get my car and pick you up at the door."

She must have heard him wrong. There was no way he was still trying to give her a ride home. "Pardon me?"

"I said, stay here while I get my car. It'll just take me a minute."

"I told you I already had a ride."

"I know, but this will be easier on everyone."

Fatigue, frustration and fear churned in Piper's belly and slammed behind her skull, and for once she wasn't concerned about hurting Brian's feelings. "I don't need a ride, Brian. How many times do I have to say it?"

"Hey, there's no need to be rude." They were in the lobby now, and Brian's tone was jovial, though his eyes flashed with irritation.

"Rude? Rude is pushing yourself on someone who isn't interested."

"Now wait just a minute." He grabbed her arm, his grip tight, his voice a quiet hiss. Anyone watching would have seen a concerned doctor offering comfort to a patient. Piper felt anything but comforted.

"Let go of my arm."

"Not until you tell me what's going on here. Do you think I'm so desperate I can't take no for an answer?"

"I don't *think* anything. I've said no to you over and over again. No to dinner. No to dates. No to a ride home. You keep ignoring me."

"Ignoring you? I've heard every word you said, and I'm not getting any clear answers to my questions. I don't think the problem is me. It's you and your inability to say what you want." He glared down into her eyes, his fingers tightening around her arm.

For the first time since she'd known him, Piper felt afraid in his presence. She shifted her weight, preparing to pull away. "Let's talk about this another time. You've got your job to go back to and I've got to get home."

"My shift just ended, so why don't we lay all our cards on the table. We went to lunch together and since then I've gotten the impression you might be interested in more."

"How can you say that? Every time you call I tell you I can't go out with you."

"Because you have too much to do. Or at least that's what you've been saying. Were you lying?"

"Of course I wasn't. It's just that…" She paused, trying to think of the right way to say what needed to be said, wishing the entire conversation could have been avoided. "I didn't want to hurt your feelings."

"Hurt my feelings? What? Are we back in high school again?"

"Brian, I am really not in the mood for this conversation."

His dark brown eyes assessed her, his gaze clinical. "Then pick a time when we *can* have this conversation."

"As far as I'm concerned there's no need. We've got nothing to discuss."

"I'm afraid I disagree." His fingers tightened fractionally, and Piper knew she'd have to make a scene if that's what was necessary to free herself. Much as she didn't want to believe it, much as she'd argued against the idea, Piper suspected that Brian McMath was more than just persistent. He might also be dangerous.

NINE

"Where'd you say she was meeting us?" Sean asked the question as he maneuvered his wheelchair out of the hospital cafeteria.

"The lobby."

"Must be close to fifteen years since I've seen her. She still play piano?"

"Plays it and teaches it."

"A woman of many talents. Sounds interesting."

Cade ignored the unspoken question and the curiosity behind it. He couldn't deny that he found Piper intriguing, but that wasn't something he planned to share with his father. "You'll see for yourself in a minute. There she is."

Dressed in dark jeans and a cream-colored sleeveless turtleneck, blond hair falling in a thick, straight line past her collar, she leaned on a crutch and glared up at the man beside her. A man who stood a little too close, his fingers curving around Piper's forearm in what looked to be a very tight grip.

Brian McMath. Cade wasn't surprised. Nor was he happy about it.

"I'll be right back, Dad." He strode across the room, watching the interplay between the two—Piper's obvious discomfort, McMath's irritation. They were at a stalemate. Or that's how it seemed until Piper shoved her arm toward Brian, using the movement to throw him off balance.

He released his grip, said something Cade couldn't hear, but that Piper didn't seem happy about.

She could handle the doctor. Cade knew it. He decided to step in anyway. "Ready to go, Piper?"

She turned, relief flooding her eyes. "I thought maybe you'd forgotten about me."

"Not possible." He slid his arm around her waist, staking a claim he had no right to, and watching the doctor for any sign of a reaction.

McMath's mouth tightened into a thin line, his gaze dropping to the spot where Cade's hand rested against Piper's waist. "I'll see you tomorrow, Piper." He offered a curt nod in Cade's direction and walked away.

"Everything okay over here?" Sean wheeled to a stop a few feet away.

"Is it?" Cade glanced down at Piper, not liking the fear that shadowed her eyes.

"Everything is fine."

"So McMath wasn't bothering you?"

"He was being a little too persistent, but nothing I couldn't handle."

She was downplaying things. Cade knew it, but

now wasn't the time to push for the truth. Not with his father watching, wide-eyed and curious. He'd find out more later, when he could speak to her alone. "Glad to hear it. You remember my father?"

"Of course. It's nice to see you again, Mr. Macalister." She eased from Cade's arm, leaning forward to shake Sean's hand, the movement revealing dark red blood on the back of her shirt and the white bandage that peeked from beneath the fabric.

"You, too. Wish the circumstances were different, though. You doing okay?"

"Nothing a few days of rest won't fix."

"You always were a tough little thing."

"A tomboy, you mean."

"Except when you played piano. Then you were a princess."

She laughed at that, the sound bright and full. "I think my brothers would argue with that, but I'll just say thank you for the compliment."

"Cade says you still play."

"I'm the pianist at Grace Christian Church."

"That's the one with the white steeple? Right outside of town?"

"Yes."

"We'll have to come hear you, won't we, Cade?"

"Sure." Though if he actually managed to get his father out of the house and to church, Cade would be surprised. He didn't bother saying as much. Just turned his attention to Piper. "Will you be okay while I get the car?"

"I'll be fine."

"If McMath comes back, stay in the lobby. Don't even think about leaving with him."

"I—"

"She's not stupid, Cade. Go get the car and stop nagging."

Cade stiffened at his father's words, but kept silent.

That surprised Piper, who'd witnessed plenty of disagreements between the two as Cade was growing up. Of course, that had been years ago. And, as Cade had been quick to point out, there wasn't much of the teenager he'd been left in the man standing before her.

"I'll be back in a minute." He pushed open the lobby door and strode toward the parking lot, long legs eating up the ground, everything about him speaking of confidence and strength.

"He's not a kid anymore, that one." Sean's voice broke into her thoughts, and Piper turned to face him.

He'd aged since she'd seen him, his red hair now snowy white, his ruddy complexion pale, his face gaunt. Only his eyes were the same—vivid green and intense. Just like his son's. "We've all grown up."

"Just took some of you longer than others. Thought that kid of mine would never come into his own. Blinked my eyes and he was a man. A good one, too. Though if you tell him I said so, I'll deny every word."

"That goes without saying." She shifted her weight, hoping to find a more comfortable stance, but the crutch bit into the underside of her arm no matter how she stood.

"Not easy with an arm and a leg out of commission, is it?"

Not nearly as bad as being confined to a wheelchair.

Piper knew Sean was thinking it, and wondered what response he expected from her. "It could be worse, Mr. Macalister."

"You could be me, you mean?"

Piper's face heated, but she didn't look away. "What I mean is that things could be worse for both of us."

He laughed, slapping his right hand against his knee. "You're still one of a kind, Piper Sinclair. And you're right. It could be worse. I could have died. I could have lost complete function on my left side. I didn't. Fact is, I could probably do more. Walk with a cane. Maybe even drive a car."

"So why don't you?"

"Good question. When I figure out an answer I'll give you one. Hey, don't look now, but your doctor friend is back."

"Where?" Despite Sean's words, Piper swung around and saw Brian bearing down on her. "Perfect."

He met her eyes. Then his gaze dropped to Sean, his face blank, as if he didn't really see either of them.

Piper braced herself anyway, sure he planned to pick their conversation up again, perhaps insist that she allow him to take her home. Instead, he drew close enough for Piper to catch a whiff of his cologne, pivoted abruptly and walked out the lobby doors.

"What's with that guy? He trying to scare you or something?"

Was he? All the things Piper had believed about Brian, all the things she'd believed about her life, seemed inaccurate; the picture she'd created of the world now filled with darkness and impenetrable shadows. "I wish I knew."

"Well, don't fret about it. If anyone can figure out what's what, Cade can. And speaking of Cade, there's the car."

Piper peered through the lobby's glass doors, saw the dark blue sedan idling at the curb. "Not an SUV, this time."

"Too hard for me to get in and out of."

As Sean spoke, Cade stepped from the car, his hair mussed, a frown pulling at the corners of his mouth. He looked concerned and frustrated, and Piper's heart had the nerve to skip a beat.

No way. There was no way she could be attracted to Cade Macalister. Not after everything he'd done to her when they were kids. Shoelaces tied together, hair pulled, plastic spiders in her music bag. The list went on and on.

But there was another list as well. One she'd never thought about until now. The times Cade had attended her piano recitals, clapping as loudly as any of her brothers, the times he'd offered to drive her to piano lessons when Seth couldn't, dinners at her parents' house when Cade had laughed at her preadolescent humor. He'd been part of the family. Another brother. Or that was how she'd seen him.

She definitely wasn't seeing him that way now.

She grimaced, stepping back as the lobby door opened.

"We're set. Need any help getting to the car?" Cade held the door open, his gaze sliding from Piper to Sean and back again.

"I'm fine. How about you, Mr. Macalister?"

"I think I can make it three yards. And call me Sean. Seems silly to be so formal now that you're an adult." He rolled his chair out the door, and Piper followed him, maneuvering out into the humid warmth of the evening.

It felt good to be outside, away from the antiseptic coolness of the hospital. As she took a deep breath of balmy air, the crutch slipped from beneath her arm and she tumbled sideways.

Cade's arm wrapped around her waist, tugging her upright before she could fall. "You okay?"

"I'm just not used to this crutch yet."

"Let me give you a hand."

"No, I—"

But he'd already pulled the crutch from her hand, his grip firm against her waist. "I saw McMath leaving as I drove up. Was he bothering you again?"

"No."

"Good. I've already called Jake. He's checking into McMath's background."

"That was quick."

"The sooner we can find out what's going on and why, the safer you'll be."

"And if you don't find anything?"

"Then we just keep looking. Someone has a bone

to pick with you. If we look hard enough, we'll find
out who and why."

Hopefully before it was too late.

The thought hung between them as Piper slid into
the backseat of the car, and she shivered despite the
warmth of the evening.

"It's going to be okay."

She glanced at Cade, and saw him watching her.
"Of course it is."

"You don't sound convinced." He handed her the
crutch, a question in his eyes and in his voice.

"I am." Or she was trying to be. Believing that everything was going to be okay when she knew
someone wanted her dead wasn't easy.

"Good. Let's get you home before Grayson sends
out a posse."

"You called him, too?"

"He called me. He wanted to know why you
weren't ready to come home yet."

"Why doesn't that surprise me?"

"Because you know how protective your brother
is."

"He means well. I try to keep that in mind."

"Then so will I." He smiled, but Piper heard the
tightness in his voice. Apparently the conversation
he'd had with Grayson wasn't nearly as cut-and-dry
as Cade was making it out to be.

He didn't give her a chance to ask. Just closed the
door and helped his father into the front seat of the car.

Piper settled back into her seat, ignoring the

twinge of pain in her shoulder, and telling herself that Cade was right. Everything would be fine.

Somehow, she couldn't quite make herself believe it.

TEN

2:00 a.m.

The glowing red numbers on the alarm clock mocked Piper's attempt at sleep. She wanted to be up moving, not lying in bed, whiling away the hours until dawn. Only the thought of Grayson sleeping on her uncomfortable sofa kept her in place. He'd seemed tired and out of sorts when he'd arrived. The last thing he needed was to be woken by Piper's restless energy.

She grimaced, turning away from the bedside clock and wincing as her aching shoulder and throbbing knee stretched with the movement. The pain was a grim reminder of what she'd been through, and Piper closed her eyes, trying to push aside the image of the dark sedan and the gun. Her heart skittered, picking up speed, galloping in her chest.

Breath heaving, she sat up and shoved aside the covers, grabbing her crutch and hopping across the room to the window. Outside, pale moonlight cast shadows across the yard and bathed the lawn in silvery light. There was beauty there and Piper wanted to enjoy it, but all she could see were the shadows that offered dark alcoves where an assassin might hide. She pulled the curtain across the window and stepped away.

As if moving away from the window would keep her from the danger that seemed to be dogging her lately.

She raised a shaky hand, pushing strands of hair from her forehead. Who wanted to harm her? Why? They were questions she'd been asking herself for hours. Questions she had yet to find answers to.

"I know You've got a plan, Lord. I know You're in control, but I wouldn't mind if You'd fill me in, give me a clue about what's going on."

There was no instant answer to her plea. At least none that Piper could hear. She grabbed her Bible from the nightstand, flipped through the well-worn pages, hoping to find comfort and insight. The house was silent around her, the rocking chair in the corner of the room the perfect place to sit and read. She'd just settled there when the phone rang, the shrill sound of it breaking the silence and scaring a few years off Piper's life.

She grabbed the receiver, hoping Grayson hadn't woken. "Hello?"

"Piper? Is that you, honey? It's Mom. We just got back to the hotel and got Grayson's message. Are you okay?"

"I'm fine. A few stitches and a wrenched knee."

"Fine? Fine!?" James Sinclair's voice boomed across the line. "Piper, you were shot! How can you say you're fine?"

"Because I am."

"Did they catch the guy who shot you?" His voice hadn't lowered and Piper held the phone away from her ear.

"Not yet. They're still looking."

"They have any ideas?"

She hesitated, knowing her father would like the answer as much as she did.

"They do. Who?"

"Wayne."

"Not our Wayne." Beth Sinclair broke into the conversation, her voice filled with the same disbelief Piper felt when she thought of Wayne trying to harm her.

"I'm afraid so."

"He's it? The only suspect?" her father sounded frustrated, and Piper could picture him pacing the room.

"They're also checking into Brian McMath's background." She didn't know if Grayson had mentioned the attempted kidnapping and the man with the tattoo, but decided she wouldn't bring it up.

"The doctor. I never did like that guy."

"That doesn't mean he's guilty of anything, Dad."

"We'll see. Mom and I will be home Friday—"

"Friday? You've got another two weeks of vacation."

"Not when our daughter is in trouble."

"But—"

"There's no sense arguing about it, honey. Dad and I contacted the airline as soon as we got Grayson's message. If we could have gotten a flight out sooner we would have."

"I can't believe you're cutting your vacation short because of me."

"Who said it's because of you? Maybe I'm just getting tired of all the sun, beaches and sand."

"Tell the truth, James, you're dying to get home so you can grill the police and find out how they're handling Piper's case."

"I won't deny it. Who's the officer in charge?"

"Jake Reed."

"Maybe I'll give him a call."

Piper didn't bother telling him not to. She knew him well enough to know he couldn't be dissuaded once he made up his mind. "I'm sure he'd be happy to talk to you. He and Cade have been working on the case together. Cade says the person responsible is someone I know, so they're checking out all the angles, trying to find someone who might have something against me."

The silence on the other end of the line was deafening.

"Mom? Dad? You still there?"

"You just quoted a man."

"Not a man, Dad. Cade Macalister."

"I don't care if it was John Wayne. You quoted him."

"And?"

"*And?* You haven't even mentioned a man's name in over a year and now you're quoting one?"

"Did you say Cade Macalister?" As always, Beth got to the crux of the issue.

"Yes. He and his father moved back to Lakeview a month or so ago."

"Really? I'm surprised I hadn't heard." Beth sounded thoughtful, her calm temperament always a perfect foil for her husband's more volatile nature.

"They're just a few blocks up from me."

"We'll have to visit when we get home. In the meantime, be careful. We'll see you Friday."

"I still wish you'd reconsider coming home early."

"Piper, if you had a daughter and she was injured, would you stay half the world away?" This time, it was James who sounded calm and reasonable.

Piper smiled and gave in to the inevitable. "No. Of course I wouldn't. Thanks for caring so much. I love you both."

"We love you, too. Is your brother around?"

"He's sleeping."

"Actually, I'm not." Grayson pushed open the door to Piper's room and stepped inside. "I heard the phone."

"Dad wants to speak with you."

While Grayson spoke to their parents, Piper sat down at the piano. A 1920 Chickering grand, it had its original ivory keys and the soft patina only time and use could bring. The legs were hand-carved and beautifully detailed, the swirling design echoed in intricate scrollwork on either side of the piano. A firm touch and rich, full tone only added to the beauty of the piece.

Piper ran her fingers over the keys, testing her shoulder as she played a chromatic scale up, then down the keyboard. She could almost hear Uncle Marcus as she worked, teasing, laughing, goading her to do more, try harder, be better.

It had been he, not her parents, who'd first noticed Piper's passion for music. She'd been young, not quite five, and still she could remember it. The family had gathered at Marcus's house, the radio playing a kind of music Piper had never heard before. She'd been too young to know that Marcus was a musician, too young to know she was listening to Mozart, but not too young to appreciate what she heard. When Grayson changed the station, she'd pitched a fit and been carried into a bedroom for a time-out. She'd still been crying when Marcus came into the room, stooped down to her level and asked why she was crying. He'd laughed when she'd told him, and he'd said something she'd never forgotten—*If you like Mozart enough to get in trouble over him, I guess I'll just have to teach you how to play him.*

"Enough!" Grayson's voice broke into Piper's thoughts and her fingers tripped over the keys, ending a song she'd barely realized she was playing. "Keep playing songs like that and we'll both be depressed."

"Sorry."

"Kind of early in the morning for piano, isn't it?" He sat on the bench beside her, nudging her over with his hip.

"I always play Genevieve when I can't sleep."

Gray winced and raked a hand through his hair. "Please tell me you did *not* name your piano."

"I didn't name her."

"That's a relief."

"Uncle Marcus did. This one is Genevieve. His Steinway was Grace. If *I'd* named them they would have been Curly and Moe."

"That figures. So, want to talk about it?"

"About why I'd choose Curly and Moe instead of Genevieve and Grace?"

"About why you're up at two in the morning."

"The same reason you're awake—Mom and Dad called."

"You were awake before the phone rang. I heard you in your room."

"I woke you?"

"I was already awake, too. Probably doing the same thing you were—trying to put together the puzzle pieces so I could see the whole picture."

"I guess you weren't successful."

"Were you?"

"No. I don't believe Brian is a stalker and I don't think Wayne would hurt me. The guy with the tattoo is the only one I can think of who'd want to harm me, and even he's a long shot."

"How so?"

"He got away. No one saw him. He's home free. Or he thinks he is. Why chance getting caught by coming after me?"

"Good question. Wish I had an answer." He paced across the room and stared out the window, his expression unreadable.

"The answer is, he wouldn't. Unless he had something to gain."

"Yeah. I was thinking the same."

Piper tapped her fingers against her thigh, waiting Grayson out, knowing he was thinking through the problem, coming up with possible solutions.

He didn't disappoint her. "The other woman, the one who was almost kidnapped, you said she was blond, about your size."

"A little heavier, but enough like me that the doctor conducting the seminar mistook her for me."

"Maybe she wasn't the only one."

"What do you mean?"

"Maybe the kidnapper made a mistake, too. Maybe *you* were his intended victim all along."

"You don't really think that's possible?"

"It's as possible as anything else we've discussed."

"Come on, Gray, I live the most boring, uneventful life imaginable. No one would want to kidnap me."

"But someone *would* want to kill you?"

He had a point, but Piper didn't want to admit it, didn't want to think that she'd been the intended victim all along. She sighed, reached for the crutch and stood. "So we're back where we started. Too many questions. No answers."

"For now, but hopefully not for long. Until then,

you need to be careful. Watch your back. Make sure you don't go places alone."

"I will."

"Good. Now, maybe we should both try to get some sleep. We've got church in the morning and I've got a meeting in the afternoon."

"On Sunday?"

"Unfortunately." He started to move away from the window and froze, staring hard out into the darkness.

"What?" Piper moved closer.

"Turn off the light."

She didn't ask why. Just flipped the switch and waited, her heart slamming against her ribs, her eyes straining to see into the darkness beyond the window. Was something moving in the trees at the edge of the yard? As she watched, the shadows seemed to shift and realign. She gasped and took an involuntary step back.

"Stay here. I'll be back in a minute."

Piper grabbed Grayson's arm before he could move away. "Are you crazy? You can't go out there."

"Sure I can." His voice was hard as granite, the fingers he used to peel Piper's fingers from his arm less than gentle.

"But what if someone's out there?"

"Then I'll find out who it is and what he wants."

"What if he has a gun? What if—"

But Grayson ignored her protests, walking to the back door, pulling it open. "Lock the door."

As if she were going to stay inside and let him face danger alone!

Piper grabbed the phone, lifted the crutch like a club and stepped into the darkness behind him.

"I told you to lock the door, not follow me." Grayson's voice was a low hiss, but he didn't turn toward her.

"Aren't you the one who always tells me there's safety in numbers?" Piper's voice was just as quiet, barely carrying over the pound of her pulse in her ears.

"Shhh!" As Grayson spoke, something crashed through the trees at the far end of the yard.

Piper screamed as a dark figure raced into the moon-bright yard.

It took only seconds for her brain to register what she was seeing—a deer. Not the masked gunman she'd expected. It took longer for her heart to sink back into her chest, for her arms to lower the crutch. By the time she did both, the deer had disappeared and silence had fallen once again.

"Well, that was exciting."

"Go in the house, Piper." This time Grayson took her by the arm and shoved her back into the house. The door slammed, the darkness inside more complete than that of the night outside.

She pushed the door back open, ready to ask Grayson what was going on, but he was gone, swallowed up by the shadows. "Gray?" Her voice wavered, whispering out into the silence. "Gray!"

The soft rustle of leaves and a muffled thump were her only answer.

"I'm calling 911." She shouted the warning as she dialed, her fingers trembling, her heart galloping in her chest.

The operator urged her back into the house, but Piper needed to find Grayson, needed to know that he was all right. Ignoring the shooting pain in her knee and the wild throb of her fear, she took one faltering step after another toward the woods.

See the
larger print
difference

in D.C. but we'll be flying back into Chicago to-morrow.''

"Did you say 'we'll'?'' Finn grabbed onto the word hopefully.

"I can't talk now, but I needed to tell you so you wouldn't worry. They're both safe and sound, praise the Lord,'' Diane said, her voice cracking slightly.

"And John? He's all right, too?''

There was a moment's hesitation. "He's fine.'' Finn heard someone say something to her in the background.

"Finn, if you're thinking about meeting the plane, I think you should reconsider. They're both pretty exhausted.''

Something in her voice didn't sound quite right. t Finn was still overwh~~~~~d by ~~~~~~~ hn and N~il we~~~

Like what you see?
Then send for TWO FREE
larger print books!

YOURS FREE!

You'll get a great mystery gift with your two free larger print books!

GET TWO FREE LARGER PRINT BOOKS!

YES! Please send me two free Love Inspired® romance novels in the larger print edition, and my free mystery gift, too. I understand that I am under no obligation to purchase anything, as explained on the back of this insert.

PLACE FREE GIFTS SEAL HERE

121 IDL EE4U   321 IDL EE46

FIRST NAME   LAST NAME

ADDRESS

APT.#   CITY

STATE/PROV.   ZIP/POSTAL CODE

Are you a current Love Inspired® subscriber and want to receive the larger print edition?

Call 1-800-221-5011 today!

▶ DETACH AND MAIL CARD TODAY! ▶

© 2004 STEEPLE HILL BOOKS

(I-LLPR-03/06)

Steeple Hill Reader Service™ — Here's How It Works:

Accepting your 2 free larger print Love Inspired® books and gift places you under no obligation to buy anything. You may keep the books and gift and return the shipping statement marked "cancel." If you do not cancel, about a month later we will send you 4 additional larger print books and bill you just $4.24 each in the U.S., or $4.99 each in Canada, plus 25¢ shipping & handling per book and applicable taxes if any.* That's the complete price, and — compared to cover prices of $5.25 each in the U.S. and $6.25 each in Canada — it's quite a bargain! You may cancel at any time, but if you choose to continue, every month we'll send you 4 more books, which you may either purchase at the discount price...or return to us and cancel your subscription.

*Terms and prices subject to change without notice. Sales tax applicable in N.Y. Canadian residents will be charged applicable provincial taxes and GST.

If offer card is missing write to: Steeple Hill Reader Service, 3010 Walden Ave., P.O. Box 1867, Buffalo, NY 14240-1867

BUSINESS REPLY MAIL
FIRST-CLASS MAIL   PERMIT NO. 717-003   BUFFALO, NY

POSTAGE WILL BE PAID BY ADDRESSEE

STEEPLE HILL READER SERVICE
3010 WALDEN AVE
PO BOX 1867
BUFFALO NY 14240-9952

NO POSTAGE
NECESSARY
IF MAILED
IN THE
UNITED STATES

ELEVEN

Despite bright moonlight, the woods behind Piper's house were dark and thick with night. Ten minutes after he'd gotten the call from dispatch, Cade eased into the blackness, the hair at the nape of his neck standing on end, every nerve in his body shouting danger. Someone was here, waiting in the darkness. Friend or foe? Cade didn't know and he had no intention of calling out or turning on his flashlight, no intention of giving whomever was there a heads-up on his location. His years in the Marines had taught him the value of waiting and of silence.

He moved cautiously, making so little noise even he couldn't hear the pad of his feet on the ground. In the distance, sirens blared, screaming an alarm to anyone listening. Cade ignored them, concentrating instead on the darkness surrounding him, on the silence that seemed to have a life of its own.

Something moved to his right, a subtle shift of air that Cade almost missed. He froze, waiting, listening, his eyes straining to see into the blackness.

Leaves crackled and a shadow separated itself from the trees, so close Cade could hear the quiet hiss of the other person's breath. He tensed, ready to spring, caught a whiff of flowers and sunshine. Piper.

"Piper?" It was barely a whisper, but she heard.

She screamed, pivoted toward him, her arm swinging up, something long and deadly looking arching into the space between them.

Cade ducked, felt a whoosh of air and lunged for Piper before she could swing again.

Hard hands gripped Piper's wrist, forcing her arm down before she could swing the crutch again. She struggled against the hold, twisting her arm, determined to free herself. Sirens blared in the distance, growing closer each second. Help would be here soon. God willing, it wouldn't be too late.

Her attacker gave a quick tug, pulling her toward him. She used the force of his movement to her advantage, lowering her head, ramming it into a rock solid chest and following the movement with a heel to his instep.

"Ow! Cool it!" He yanked her closer, wrapping an arm around both of hers. "It's me. Cade."

"Cade? You scared ten years off my life."

"Ditto." His voice was tight, and tension poured off him in waves.

"What—"

"Shhh. Someone's coming." He stepped back, pulling her with him, sliding deeper into the shadows.

She heard it then—the quiet crackle of dead leaves

underfoot—and went as still and silent as Cade. A flash of blue through the trees told Piper that a police cruiser had arrived. She wanted to grab Cade's hand and run toward it. Only the thought of a gunman hidden somewhere in the trees kept her from moving.

"Piper!"

She recognized the voice immediately, opened her mouth to call out to Grayson.

Cade's hand slid across her jaw, settled against her lips. "Quiet. Let's not give away our location. Just in case."

In case what? In case a gunman *was* hiding in the woods? Or in case Grayson was the gunman? The last was so ludicrous Piper shook her head and pulled away from Cade's hand. Still, she was silent, fear for Grayson, for herself, for Cade, sealing her lips and keeping her in place.

Someone moved past. Grayson. The height and breadth of his shoulders obvious even in the darkness.

"Grayson! What's going on, man?" Cade's voice was so loud, Piper nearly jumped out of her skin.

Grayson whirled toward his voice, pivoting one way and then another, apparently unable to see them in the shadows. "Cade? Is that you?"

"Yeah."

"We've got to find Piper."

"She's safe."

"Thank God."

"What happened out here?"

"Someone was watching the house. I came out to

meet him and got knocked over the head for my efforts."

"Are you hurt?" Piper sounded breathless. She felt breathless, terror squeezing the air from her lungs and making her weak.

"Nothing a couple of aspirin won't cure. Are you okay?"

"I'm fine. The only person I ran into out here was Cade."

"You wouldn't have run into anyone if you'd stayed in the house like I'd told you."

"What's done is done. Let's get her back to the house." Cade's voice rumbled close to Piper's ear, his arm sliding from her waist, his hand linking with hers and tugging her toward her yard.

"Looks like your backup is here." As Grayson spoke, twin beams of light speared the darkness of the woods and a disembodied voice shouted into the night.

"Freeze. Keep your hands where I can see them."

"I'm Grayson Sinclair. My sister is the one who called for help." His voice was weary, his face pale in the beam of the flashlight.

The second light illuminated Cade's face, then flashed onto Piper. "Everyone's okay?"

"Fine. So let's get organized and see if we can find our perp." Cade's voice was terse, and he dropped Piper's hand, moving closer to the uniformed officers.

She followed, feeling vulnerable despite the men surrounding her.

"Jamison, you want to escort Ms. Sinclair back to the house?" Cade said to the older of the two officers.

"No. He doesn't. That would be a waste of time and manpower. I can go back to the house myself."

"There's only one person the guy we're looking for is after—you. Letting you walk back to the house alone will be like handing him what he wants on a silver platter."

"You really don't think he's hanging around? Not with all the lights, the people. He'd be a fool."

"Foolish is as good a description as any. That, or desperate."

Desperate?

What could she possibly know, possibly have, that could make someone desperate enough to come after her?

"All right." She started toward the officer, stopping short when Cade grabbed her hand and tugged her back. "Are you planning on staying in the house this time?"

Piper looked up into his eyes, dark pools in the pre-dawn light. "Yes."

"Good." He smiled, leaned forward. She barely had time to register the warmth of his lips against her forehead before he turned and walked away.

"Ready, Miss Sinclair?" The officer shifted from foot to foot, his impatience obvious.

"Sure. Of course."

And she *was* ready to go home.

What she wasn't sure she was ready for was Cade

Macalister. Having him around was like having another brother. Only worse.

Her brothers were annoyingly protective, but they didn't threaten her equilibrium, didn't make her wonder if all her talk of not wanting or needing another man in her life was just that—talk.

Hadn't she decided not to date? Hadn't she decided that she preferred to spend her time in more constructive and less irritating ways? And why was that? It was because she'd realized how useless dating was. The men she'd been out with were either wimpy and whiny, or arrogant jerks. Finding a good man was more trouble than it was worth. Wasn't it?

If God wanted her married, He'd have to deliver a groom—fully dressed in wedding finery—to her doorstep. Otherwise, she had more important things to do with her time.

With that thought in mind, she stepped inside the house and shut the door firmly behind her.

TWELVE

Piper brewed and discarded three pots of coffee while she waited, spent endless minutes praying that the search team was safe and would have worn a path across the wood floor of the kitchen if using the crutch hadn't hampered her pacing.

By the time the sound of voices outside the back door reached her ears, she was on edge and exhausted, her shoulder and knee aching, her head throbbing.

She hurried forward, but the door swung open before she could reach it and Grayson stepped inside, his gray eyes searching for her. "Where's your house key?"

"Hanging on the hook by the front door."

"Who else has a copy of it?" The question was abrupt and unexpected.

Piper scrambled for an answer as Cade moved into the room behind Grayson.

"You do. Dad and Mom. Gabriella. Tristan."

"Anyone else?" Grayson raked a hand through his hair, revealing a deep blue lump on his temple.

"Gray! That looks awful. Let me get you some ice."

"That can wait. This can't. Does anyone else have your key?"

"No."

"You're sure?" Cade moved past her, grabbed a mug from the counter and poured coffee into it.

"Yes. I had the keys made when I moved in. I remember exactly who I gave them to."

"Did you have the locks on the house changed at the same time?" Cade handed the cup to Grayson and grabbed a second for himself.

"No. I didn't see any need to. Why? What's going on?"

"We found this in the woods behind your house." Cade held up a clear plastic bag with an old-fashioned skeleton key in it. "We tried it in the back door. It worked."

"It was in the woods?"

"Right near the place where your Peeping Tom and I had a run-in." Grayson eased into a chair, his skin leached of color.

"A run-in? I thought you said he knocked you out."

"He did. After I tackled him to the ground. I'm not sure what he was holding in his hand, but it packed a wallop." Grayson touched the swollen knot on his head, and Piper grabbed a bag of frozen corn from the freezer and handed it to him.

"Did you find anything else?"

"Unfortunately, no." Cade took a swig of coffee

and put the mug back down on the counter. "Maybe we'll get some prints off this key."

"I have a feeling that won't be the case." Piper leaned against the counter, all the adrenaline that had coursed through her while she waited suddenly gone.

"It's worth a try. Especially since it's all we've got." Grayson pressed the bag of corn against the lump on his head and grimaced.

"It's not all we've got. Jake put in a call to the state police. They're lending us a sketch artist. We'll get a composite of the kidnapper's tattoo, get it out to the press and hopefully be having a chat with the guy in the next few days."

"*If* someone comes forward with information about him." Grayson's frustration was obvious, his expression grim.

"We're posting a reward. If appealing to people's better nature doesn't work, appealing to their greed might. I'll give you a ring tomorrow, let you know when the artist is coming." Cade rubbed a hand along his jaw. "I know I don't need to say this, but you need to get the locks changed. Sooner rather than later."

"I will."

"Good. Now, I'd better head out. Jake is waiting for me at the station."

Piper followed him to the door, opened it to gray dawn and overcast skies. "I can't believe the sun is coming up. I don't feel like I slept at all."

"Did you?"

"Actually, no. Too much on my mind." And that was probably a good thing. If she'd been sleeping, if Grayson had been, the person waiting out in the woods might have snuck into the house without either of them hearing him. She shivered, rubbing her hands up and down her arms.

"You're cold. Go wrap up in a warm blanket and try to sleep. Maybe it'll be easier now that the sun is coming up."

"Dawn chases away nightmares, but it can't do the same to reality."

What could Cade say to that? He knew only too well how harsh reality could be. He reached for her hands, pulling them from her arms and tugging her forward. It felt right to wrap his arms around her, to absorb the fine trembling of her muscles. "Things are going to be okay."

"Are they? Because right now it doesn't feel like it."

Any reassurance would be false, any platitudes a lie. Cade leaned back, looked down into Piper's eyes. "I won't lie and tell you you're safe. Until we catch this guy, there aren't any guarantees. But God is here. He's in control."

"I know. You're right. I just…"

"What?"

"I was going to say 'want my life back the way it was.'"

"But you don't?"

"Of course I do." Didn't she? She wanted safety, she wanted security, but did she want the whirlwind of activity that kept her running from dawn to dusk each day?

"Piper, do you have any aspirin?" Grayson stepped from the kitchen, his brow furrowing as he caught sight of his sister standing in Cade's arms.

She blushed, stepped away from Cade. "In the cupboard above the fridge."

"I'll see you both later." Cade stepped outside and pulled the door shut behind him.

"What's up with the two of you?" Grayson's voice pulled Piper's attention from the closed door and the man who'd disappeared behind it.

"Nothing."

"It looked like a lot more than nothing."

"Did it? Come on, I'll get you some aspirin."

"Avoiding the subject is just going to make me more curious."

He wasn't the only one who was curious, but Piper had no intention of letting Grayson know that. "I'm not avoiding it. I'm exhausted. It's been a long day. I don't have the energy to move, let alone get into a discussion about Cade."

"You're right. Sorry." But he didn't look sorry as he took the aspirin Piper handed him and swallowed it down with coffee. "Church starts in less than six hours. Let's try to get some sleep before then."

As if she *could* sleep.

But Piper retreated to her room anyway, worry, fear, frustration all clamoring for attention in her mind. She tossed her crutch onto the bed, lowered herself into the rocking chair and grabbed her Bible. She didn't open it, though. Just sat in silence as grayish light peeked through the slats of the shades and bathed the room in the new day.

"Do you see her yet?" Sean's voice cut through the preservice hubbub, and the woman sitting in front of him turned with a frown.

"No." Cade kept to a one-word response, hoping to discourage his father. It had been a long sleepless night. Exhaustion had come and gone. Now he was just frustrated. Frustrated with his inability to track down whoever was after Piper. Frustrated with his father's sudden and endless chatter. Frustrated with his own frustration.

"You think she decided to stay home? That's not her at the piano. Maybe—"

"For someone who has spent a year and a half using grunts and one-word answers to communicate you sure are chatty, Dad."

Sean shot a look in Cade's direction, his eyes clear, his mind as sharp as ever despite the stroke and its aftermath. "Long night?"

"Too long."

"You'll get the guy, Cade."

"Sure we will. But will we get him before he does more damage?" The question had been haunting Cade since he'd walked out of Piper's house—voicing it now didn't make him feel better. He should be at the station, checking out leads, but Jake had sent him home at eight, telling him to nap before the sketch artist arrived at noon.

And Dad had picked today to insist on going to church.

Which was fine. Cade had missed attending services in the month since they'd moved to Lakeview.

"Can we squeeze in here?" Grayson Sinclair's voice broke into Cade's thoughts and he looked up, meeting Gray's eyes and then Piper's. She looked tired and pale, her bandaged shoulder peeking out from the sundress she wore.

"Sure. There's plenty of room." Sean managed to slide over and Cade followed suit.

"Thanks." Grayson stepped back and motioned for his fiancée to slide in. "Go ahead, Maria."

"I prefer to sit on the end. You know that, Gray."

Grayson's face darkened. "Piper needs room to stretch her leg."

"Then maybe we should sit in a different pew. There's one near the front. And look, Betsy Oliver is there. Weren't we going to talk to her about listing your condo?"

"We've got a few months before we have to—"

"It's okay, Gray. Go ahead. I'll meet you here when the service is over." Piper's exhaustion seeped through her words.

"Thanks, Piper." Maria turned to smile at her future sister-in-law, the flashing of white teeth doing little to warm her expression. "Men just don't seem to understand how much time and effort it takes to plan a wedding and a marriage. Come on, Grayson, if we hurry we'll have a chance to speak to Betsy before the service begins." She grabbed Grayson's arm and tugged him away without bothering to say goodbye.

Piper slid into the pew beside Cade, sending a smile in his direction. It lit her face, brightening pallid skin and fatigue-rimmed eyes. "I wasn't expecting to see you two here this morning."

"We weren't sure if we'd see you, either. Did you get any rest?" Cade's eyes scanned her face, seeming to take in every detail.

"I'm not sure I know what that is anymore." She laughed, but there was tightness to the sound.

"Things will be better soon. The state's sketch artist will be here this afternoon. We'll get the composite. Get things moving along."

"What time? Grayson's got a meeting this afternoon and my car—"

"Is still being gone over with a fine-tooth comb. Don't worry. Jake's arranged to have the guy come to you."

"That was nice of him."

And probably a lot more trouble than Jake had made it out to be. But that was something Piper didn't need to know or worry about. "He wants to get this guy. We all do."

"Which guy? We don't even know who it is or what he wants."

"So maybe we'll find out from the guy with the tattoo."

She ran a hand through her hair, the straight, blond strands falling around her face in a silken curtain that concealed her expression. "Maybe. Is there anything else? Any other leads?"

"Now's not the time to discuss it."

"So there are."

"Jake and I will fill you in this afternoon."

She might have pushed for more, but the organist began playing, and Piper forced herself to settle back against the pew. She was used to being up front playing piano, not sitting idle during this part of the service. Maybe that's why she felt antsy. Or maybe it was the feeling she couldn't shake, the one that told her someone was watching.

She glanced around. Of course someone was watching. Half the congregation was sneaking peeks in her direction. Obviously, news of her troubles had spread.

Pastor Ben Avery's words filled the sanctuary, his voice strong and firm as he read from Matthew 19. The story of the rich young man took on life and meaning as Ben explained its history and significance. Piper tried to concentrate as he spoke of choices, of direction, of lives focused on the wrong things, but her muscles were tight with anxiety, and she shifted again, trying to find one person who stood out from the crowd, someone who might be staring a bit more intently.

"What's wrong?" The words were a warm breath against her ear, the hand that cupped the back of Piper's neck strong and firm.

"Nothing. I just feel like I'm being watched." She whispered the words, hoping Cade would laugh them off, tell her she was paranoid, convince her that there was no enemy hiding among her friends.

He didn't. His hand slid from her neck, and he shifted subtly, letting his arm drop around her shoulder as his eyes scanned the congregation. "Doesn't look like anyone is watching, but that doesn't mean much."

His words did little to ease Piper's tension and by the time the sermon wound to an end her head throbbed with fatigue and anxiety.

She stood for the benediction, wobbling a little as she balanced on one leg, but still managing a smile as one person after another approached to offer sympathy and support.

"There's McMath," Cade's voice rumbled near her ear and Piper caught a quick glimpse of Brian as he hurried through the departing congregation. He didn't seem to notice her. Which only made her sure that he did.

Wayne was darting through the crowd as well, his gaze on the floor, his face set. She knew he was avoiding her, and wished she could allow it, but she needed an answer regarding the antiques and now was as good a time as any to get it.

"Wayne!"

He kept going.

"Wayne!" she called again, and this time he glanced her way, backtracking a few steps.

"Feeling better?"

"Yes. Listen, you were supposed to call me. I really need to get with you about those—"

"I *will* call you. Tomorrow. Better yet, why don't I stop by the college around lunchtime? We'll talk then." His words were brisk, his eyes going from Piper to Cade.

"I'd rather speak with you today. I'm supposed to meet with Miriam on Wednesday. We're discussing appraisals and insurance. I want to give her the complete list then. If we can't—"

"We'll talk tomorrow." He cut her off again, this time turning away and losing himself in the crowd.

"Is he always like that?" Cade's eyes were sharp-edged, his gaze following Wayne as he hurried away.

Was he? A year ago Piper would have said no. Now she wasn't sure. "He's been under a lot of stress lately."

"And you haven't?"

She didn't have a chance to answer.

"Piper!" John Sweeny stepped from the throng. "I just heard the news. Are you all right?"

"Yes."

"You look worn out. The past few days haven't been easy on you."

"You're right about that, Mr. Sweeny."

"Do the police have any idea who is responsible?"

"Not yet, but I'll be working with a sketch artist after church."

"A sketch artist? So, you saw someone last night?"

"No, I—"

"The police will release the sketch and the information when they're ready," Cade cut in, his hand on Piper's shoulder, his gaze on John.

"And you would be...?"

"Cade Macalister. I'm with the Lakeview Sheriff's Department."

"I don't recall seeing you before."

"I haven't been in town long."

"I see. I'm John Sweeny, CEO of Music Makers."

"Piper's mentioned you. You were Marcus's friend."

"And business partner. We founded Music Makers together. He had the dream. I had the know-how." John's smile didn't reach his eyes.

"You're an accountant." It wasn't a question, and the fact that Cade knew could only mean one thing—Wayne and Brian weren't the only people being investigated.

"That's right. I've always been good at crunching numbers. Marcus and I were a perfect business match. Music Makers misses him. I miss him." He cleared his throat, picked an imaginary piece of lint off his suit. "I've got to go. Call me if you need anything, Piper."

"Thanks."

Cade watched him go, his expression unreadable.

"What are you thinking?"

"About?" He met Piper's gaze.

"About Mr. Sweeny."

"Nothing."

"Then why were you looking at him like he was a bug under a microscope?"

"Because he knows you, and as far as I'm concerned, everyone who knows you is a suspect until we prove otherwise."

"He's known me since the day I was born. He'd never hurt me."

"Neither would McMath. Neither would Wayne. Neither would the guy with the tattoo. Yet someone *is* trying to harm you." He said it without rancor, his gaze scanning the crowd, his hand still on Piper's shoulder, warm, comforting and familiar.

She was relieved when Grayson arrived, Maria close by his side. "Ready to go?"

"Sure. Just let me find Nancy. I want to thank her for filling in at the piano today."

"We don't want to rush you, dear, but Grayson and I both have appointments this afternoon. We really need to leave now. Not five minutes from now." Maria linked her arm through Gray's, her voice saccharine sweet.

Piper swallowed back resentment and the harsh retort that danced on the tip of her tongue. "Fine. I'll call Nancy when I get home."

"Go find your friend, Piper. Dad and I can give you a ride home," Cade chimed.

"I—"

"Perfect. Let's go, Grayson. We've got to hurry if I'm going to make my lunch appointment."

"We can wait a few minutes." The words were quiet, firm and brooked no argument.

Maria bristled at Grayson's side, her lips pinching in a look Piper recognized.

"It's okay, Grayson. I'll ride with Cade." She had some questions she wanted to ask him anyway. This would be the best time to do it. "Let me just find Nancy and we can head out."

"I'll go with you. You don't mind waiting here do you, Dad?"

Sean glanced away from the woman he'd been speaking to and shook his head. "I'm fine."

Piper thought about telling Cade that he could stay with his father, but she still felt hunted, still wondered if her enemy stood nearby, watching. "All right. I think she's standing by the piano."

THIRTEEN

Seated sideways on the backseat of Cade's car, her leg resting on Sean's folded suit jacket, Piper felt safe for the first time in hours. She chuckled as Sean described his son's first-grade attempt to bribe his teacher with apples, his third-grade superhero leap from the garage roof, his fifth-grade attempt at investigative reporting.

By the time they turned onto Piper's street, she was laughing so hard tears slid down her cheeks. "So the police actually carted him off to jail?"

"In handcuffs. Of course, that was after they called me and asked what to do with him."

"Hey! You never told me that." Cade pulled into Piper's driveway and turned to face his father.

"Would have ruined the impact. I figured if you were really going to be an investigative reporter you better learn what happens when you break the law to get a story."

"So you let me sit in jail for half the day?"

"One hour, ten minutes and fifteen seconds to be

exact. I was outside the police department the entire time, pacing and worrying."

"I had no idea."

"Of course you didn't. That would have—"

"Ruined the impact." As he spoke, Cade surveyed the area around Piper's house. The woods that lined the edges of the yard were thick with spring growth. It would be easy for an assassin to hide there, undetected in the shadows of foliage and high grass. A flash of light reflected off metal, a hint of movement in the undergrowth, the sway of grass that should have been motionless—any of those things would have warned of trouble. Cade saw none of them.

Sean had fallen silent, his head cocked, his eyes on the towering maple trees. "Looks safe enough."

"Looks can be deceiving."

"I was thinking the same."

"Stay with Piper while I check the perimeter. If someone's here, I'll know it."

"What's going on?" Piper leaned forward, her hair sliding in a thick curtain along her cheek. Cade's fingers itched to brush the silky strands away from her face.

"Just being cautious."

"Do you think someone is out there?"

Did he? Cade surveyed the yard again, felt nothing that warned him they were in danger. "No, but it's always better to play it safe."

He stepped out of the car, listening for the click of a gun's safety being released, and heard nothing but the quiet thump of his heart. Somewhere in the distance a car engine burst to life, a child shrieked with excitement, a crow cawed an irritated warning. The sounds of a normal Sunday afternoon in Lakeview.

Cade walked the perimeter of the yard, looking for matted grass or broken branches, some sign that someone had been there. He checked the house, too, jiggling windows, trying the doors. Finally satisfied, he walked back to the car and pulled open Piper's door. "Everything looks good."

"I'll feel better about coming home when I have an alarm system and a dog keeping things safe while I'm gone."

Cade didn't tell her that nothing could keep her safe if someone was determined to harm her, that home wasn't the only place she was vulnerable. He'd seen enough victims during his years as an MP, enough violence and senseless death to keep him up late into the night.

"Are you two heading home? Or would you like to come in for something to drink?" Her eyes were clear gray and shimmering with worry.

"Coffee would be good. Are you up for it, Dad?"

"Sure."

Cade extended his hand, offering Piper help out of the car before walking around and offering his father the same. "I'll get your chair."

"Don't bother. I'll use my cane."

Cade didn't point out that Sean had adamantly refused to use the cane since it was given to him three months ago. Instead he pulled it from the trunk of the car and handed it to his father, looking up as a red Corvette sped into sight. It pulled up to the curb and the door flew open, a tall, lean man stepping out. He glanced up at Cade, his eyes hidden by dark glasses, his hair pulled back in a ponytail that looked as long and thick as Piper's. "This the Sinclair residence?"

"Who's asking?"

"Ty Windrunner. I work for Virginia State Police." He flashed his ID.

"The sketch artist."

"Right."

"You're early."

"I was told afternoon. It's afternoon." He grabbed a sketchpad from the seat of the car and closed the door.

"No computer?"

"Good old-fashioned paper and pencil." He opened the trunk, pulled out a briefcase and headed toward Piper, who'd pushed the front door open and was standing in the threshold.

"Ms. Sinclair?"

"Yes."

"Ty Windrunner. I hope I'm not here at a bad time." The words were kind, the tone cold.

"Not at all. Come in, Mr. Windrunner."

"Ty. It's easier on the tongue. I called Sheriff Reed when I hit town. He should be here in a few minutes." He pulled off his glasses, glanced around the room. "Is there a table where we can work?"

"In the kitchen. Would you like coffee? A soda?"

"Nothing. Thanks." The words were abrupt, his dark eyes looking past Piper toward the kitchen. "In there?"

"Yes."

He brushed past her, impatient to begin.

That was fine with Piper. The sooner the sketch was finished and in the hands of the media, the happier she would be.

It took an hour. In that time Ty managed to create a sketch so like the snake tattoo Piper had seen that looking at it made her shudder. She scooted her chair back from the table and stood, distancing herself from the drawing Ty held out to her.

"That's it." Even the arm and hand were the same, thick and broad, the snake coiled and ready to strike.

"You're sure?" Jake Reed leaned against the kitchen counter, nursing a cup of coffee and looking like he'd gotten as little sleep as Piper.

"Yes. Down to the last detail."

Cade stepped closer to Ty, his eyes scanning the drawing. "It's a unique tattoo."

He exchanged a look with Jake, a grim smile turning up the corners of his mouth. "Someone is going to recognize it."

"Then I guess we'd better get it to the media."

"And I guess I'm done here." Ty grabbed his brief-case and sketchpad. "Nice meeting you, Piper."

"You, too." She started to follow him to the door, but he shook his head.

"I'll show myself out."

She let him, too tired to do more than send a half-hearted wave in his direction.

"Any more coffee in here?" Sean shuffled into the room, his eyes bright with curiosity as he approached the table and looked down at the sketch. "Wow. That's quite a tattoo."

"I was just saying the same thing." Cade picked up the sheet of paper. "We'll be getting calls within an hour of this airing."

"And if we don't?" All three men turned to look at Piper, and she shrugged. "He might not be from around here. And even if he is we don't know that someone will turn him in."

"Then we'll keep looking. There's information somewhere, someone who knows something. It's just a matter of time." Jake put down his cup, straightened. "I've got to get back to the station. We've got a few leads we're still trying to track down."

"Like?" Piper's question stopped Jake before he could walk from the kitchen and he turned to look at her.

"Cade hasn't told you?"

"There hasn't been time." Cade shrugged.

Jake nodded and continued. "Wayne is forty thousand dollars in debt. He's behind on his mortgage. Looks like he needs money in a bad way."

"I didn't realize things were that bad."

"You knew about the debt?" Cade's tension was obvious in the tightness of his jaw.

"I knew he owed money for the medical treatment Marcus was getting."

"Did you know Marcus's life insurance company won't pay out? That they're investigating?" This time, it was Jake who spoke, his gaze hard.

"Wayne mentioned there was a problem."

"More than a problem. They're trying to prove suicide. The investigator thinks it's odd that on the one day out of a hundred that Wayne was out of town, Marcus had an accident and died."

"Accidents happen." But it did seem an odd coincidence. One Piper hadn't thought about before.

"Was your uncle suicidal, Piper? You knew him as well as anyone. Maybe understood him more than most. What do you think?" Cade looked relaxed, but something told Piper he was anxious to hear her answer.

And what could she say? Marcus loved his music, his work. With ALS stealing both away, he might have felt depressed; might have believed he was a burden to those who loved him. "I don't know. He didn't seem it when we spoke, or when I visited, but it's hard to know what's in someone else's heart or mind."

"He never gave you any reason to think he was desperate?"

"No. Just the opposite. He was always talking about fighting the disease. Always mentioning new treatments, new experimental drugs. I'd say he was hopeful that he'd be cured, but that might be stretching it."

Cade exchanged a look with Jake, passing some secret message that Piper couldn't decipher.

"What? What are the two of you thinking?"

"Your uncle's death was ruled an accident. Wayne and your uncle's housekeeper both testified to the fact that Marcus liked to go out on the dock every morning. It was a ritual." Jake spoke quietly, his words carefully measured.

"It was. Everyone knew it."

"And when the housekeeper arrived that morning and Marcus wasn't at the house, she went down to the dock, saw the wheelchair tipped onto its side, Marcus in the lake."

"The dock was old. A few of the planks were loose. It looked like one of the wheelchair's wheels had gotten stuck. That Uncle Marcus had been trying to maneuver around the spot and the chair had fallen over." Piper filled in details that had haunted her for months after Marcus's death. That *still* haunted her.

"Right." Jake raked a hand through his hair. "Looked enough like an accident to be one. No sign of foul play. No sign of a struggle. Bits of wood in Marcus's palms as if he'd been trying to pull himself out. That's why the medical examiner didn't rule it a suicide at the time."

"I remember." The thought of her uncle, struggling to free himself from the lake, made her light-headed.

Jake's eyes narrowed as he watched her and she knew she must have lost what little color she had. He put a hand on her arm. "Sorry. You didn't need the reminder. I'm just making a point. And the point is, your uncle had no enemies. He was well-liked. Even loved. The only two people who stood to gain something from his death were you and Wayne. You were teaching a class at the time and Wayne was out of town. We investigated, but in the end we agreed with the medical examiner—Marcus's death was an accident."

"And now you're not sure."

"No, we're not. So we're looking into anyone who had dealings with both you and your uncle. That includes Wayne, Miriam Bradshaw and John Sweeny."

"I thought you were investigating Brian McMath."

"Him, too." Cade spoke this time, his eyes redrimmed with fatigue. "We've learned a few interesting things about McMath."

"Really?" Piper decided sitting down for the news might be best, and she lowered herself into a chair. "Like what?"

"Like you're not the first woman to complain about him. He's had a few incidents at work. Nothing anyone will label harassment, but several women have said he won't take no for an answer. One went so far as to quit and find work at a hospital in Lynchburg. She said, and this is a direct quote, he was creepy."

"So maybe what's happening to me has nothing to do with Uncle Marcus."

Jake shrugged. "We don't know, but we plan to find out. Which is why I've got to get this composite to the station. We'll make copies. Start distributing it. Call me if you have any questions or concerns."

"Thanks." She stood and walked out into the living room with him, pain spearing through her shoulder and knee as she moved.

Jake pulled the door open, pausing before he walked out into bright sunlight. "You getting your locks changed?"

"Yes."

"And Cade says you're getting a dog."

"That's right."

"Good. I'll have men patrolling your street, but if anything makes you nervous call it in. No sense taking chances."

She didn't tell him that everything made her nervous lately, just smiled and nodded. "Thanks, Jake. I appreciate all you're doing."

"Wish I could do more. Or at least do it faster." He saluted and headed for his car.

"We should probably get out of here, too." Cade stepped up behind Piper and rested a hand on her un-injured shoulder.

She glanced back, her eyes wide and dark in a too-pale face. The past few days had drained her. Cade knew it. Wished he could change it.

"I can make sandwiches if you want to stay for lunch. You and your father must be getting hungry."

"We're fine."

"Speak for yourself, son. I wouldn't mind a little something." Sean shuffled into the room, his right leg dragging, his left hand clutching the cane.

"Dad—"

"It's okay. I wouldn't have offered if I hadn't wanted you to stay." She smiled, gestured to the couch. "Go ahead and have a seat. I'll see what I have to offer."

"I'll give you a hand." Cade followed her toward the kitchen, shooting a look at his father as he passed.

Sean looked smug, his self-satisfied smile grating along Cade's overly raw nerves. Apparently his father had some twisted idea about matchmaking. Cade didn't have time or energy to waste telling him why now was not an appropriate time for it.

"Sorry about this." He spoke as he stepped into the kitchen behind Piper.

"About what?"

"Infringing on your afternoon. Dad knows better."

"I did offer, Cade."

"Because it seemed like the thing to do? Or because you really wanted the company?"

She was silent for a moment, then shrugged. "A little of both. I'm not really up to company, but I'm also not sure I want to be alone. I keep thinking about that key you found last night, wondering if there are other copies of it."

"I can replace the locks for you."

"Gray is going to do it when he gets back. I'll feel a lot better when it's done. Does your Dad like chicken Caesar salad? That's about all I've got the ingredients for."

"Dad's not picky."

"Yes, I am." Sean's voice drifted in from the living

room. "Chicken Caesar sounds great. Cade can make it. You can come in here and keep me company."

"Thanks, Sean, but I'll make the salad. I'm not sure I trust your son to do a good job."

"He's a pretty good cook. Give him a chance to show off his skills. You'll be impressed."

"I don't think he cares about impressing me." She spoke as she grabbed a bowl from the cupboard.

Cade tugged it from her hands. "What makes you think that?"

"What?"

"That I don't want to impress you."

"Why would you? We've known each other so long I don't think either of us could impress the other."

"Now that's where you're wrong." He opened the refrigerator, saw a bag of precooked chicken and handed it to Piper. "You've already impressed me."

"With what? My ability to get into trouble?"

"With your ability to stay cool under fire. The last couple days have been rough, but you just keep going."

"Is there a choice?"

"There's always a choice."

"Not for me." The words were matter-of-fact, and Cade knew they were meant to be. Dressed in her navy blue sundress and heels, piano earrings dangling from her ears, Piper looked cool and calm, though Cade suspected she was anything but.

"Even for you. Grayson wouldn't mind having you stay with him. Then there's Tristan. He lives close by, right?"

"Yes. But you already knew that. I'm sure you've checked out everyone in my family."

"Jude is in New York. You could—"

"No. I couldn't. I've got too much to do here. Finals. The Music Makers book. I've got a meeting Wednesday to discuss that and the exhibit Miriam and I are putting together. Appraisals need to be done and we have to set that up."

"None of that will matter if something happens to you, Piper."

She looked up from the salad she was sprinkling with Parmesan, the fear she'd been hiding flashing in her eyes. "I know."

He wouldn't say any more, wouldn't push her to go into hiding. Not when he knew leaving town was no guarantee of her safety.

"Okay. This is ready." Her smile was bright and brittle. "Do you want soda, coffee or water with it?"

"Water will do for me." Sean's voice drifted from the living room again, and Piper grabbed a glass from the cupboard and a bottle of water from the fridge. Her hands trembled as she poured, but Cade didn't point it out. Instead, he slid the tray from her grasp before she could lift it, offering help in the only way he could.

And it wasn't enough. Not nearly.

She was vulnerable here in her vintage house with its old windows and outdated locks. He knew it and was helpless to do anything about it. Even with Grayson here, even with a dog, an alarm system and new locks, there was no assurance that Piper would be safe. That bothered Cade. What bothered him more was that she trusted him, trusted Jake, trusted her brother to keep her safe. None of them could. They could try. They could follow every lead, question every suspect, but until they had proof, until they knew for sure who was after her, there was little they could do to make sure the guy didn't strike again.

Except pray. And Cade had every intention of spending a lot of time doing just that.

FOURTEEN

Grayson arrived an hour later, his suit jacket flung over his shoulder, exhaustion etching fine lines around his mouth. He greeted the Macalisters, then turned to Piper. "I hear the sketch artist did a good likeness of the tattoo."

"Better than good. Jake said it'll be on the news tonight."

"So he told me. You look beat, sis."

"I was just thinking the same about you."

"An hour to put these locks in and we'll both get some rest."

"Let me give you a hand and it'll take half the time." Cade picked up one of the locks Grayson had set on the end table.

"I appreciate it. I've got stuff for the windows, too." Grayson held up a paper bag and Piper grabbed it, peering inside.

"What were you planning to do? Nail the windows shut?"

"Close. We'll drill a few holes through the windowpane and slip nails in when we're done. It's a cheap fix and effective." Gray pulled the bag from her hand, set it on the couch.

"I can help." Piper picked up the bag.

"You're forgetting your stitches." Cade smiled that look-at-my-dimple smile that played havoc with Piper's heart, and grabbed the bag, passing it to his father. "Here, Dad, why don't you try your hand at this?"

Sean looked surprised and pleased to be given the task. Still, Piper wasn't sure it was fair to ask him. She'd do just as well with her injuries as he would with only one hand. "I can—"

Too late. All three men were hurrying to their tasks. Which left Piper standing in the middle of the room alone. It shouldn't have bothered her. It did.

Despite the fact that she was used to living alone, that she *liked* living alone, that she cherished what little time she had when she wasn't surrounded by students, co-workers, family or friends, she really didn't want to be alone right now. Not when alone meant time to think about the moments before she'd been shot, the masked gunman, the Peeping Tom. But telling that to any of the three men working so diligently to secure her house was something she couldn't bring herself to do.

She moved down the hall toward her room, catching sight of Cade working on the back door, then Sean struggling with a window in the office. When she offered to help, he shooed her away with a gruff, "Get some rest."

And maybe rest *was* what she needed. Maybe

sleep would improve her mood and her outlook. She locked the bedroom door, changed into sweats and an oversize T-shirt with neon green and orange smiley faces printed across the front, and lowered herself onto the bed, wincing at the burning pain in her shoulder and throbbing ache in her knee.

She could hear voices, the deep rumble she associated with her father and brothers. Only it wasn't her father and brothers in the house. Sure, Grayson was there, but so were Cade and Sean. Cade, who'd changed more than Piper ever could have imagined, turning from an annoying teenage boy into a...

A man. An attractive one. But that wasn't the worst part of the transformation. "Attractive" Piper could resist. Hadn't she resisted Brian? And Rick what's-his-name, who'd rented the house across the street for a few months? And Barry? Piper could think of five very handsome men who'd asked her out in the year since she'd decided to give up on relationships. She'd turned them all down.

No, handsome wasn't the problem. It was nice that was going to be her downfall. Cade was nice. Diplomatic. Not pushy, though he certainly knew how to get his way when he wanted to. He cared. It was in his eyes and his voice. He could be counted on. And he was tough. The kind of guy a woman wanted by her side in the middle of the night when the wind howled outside and every noise seemed a sinister warning.

"Piper? Are you okay?" As if her thoughts had

conjured him, Cade's voice drifted through the closed door. A gentle tap against the wood followed.

She hobbled to the door, pulled it open. "I'm fine."

"You're pale." His finger traced a path down her cheek. "And you're wincing every time you move your arm."

"My shoulder's a little sore."

"A little?"

"A lot."

"How about your knee?"

"I haven't made up my mind."

"About whether it hurts?"

"About whether it hurts more than my shoulder." She tried to smile, knew she failed miserably.

"Why don't I get you one of those pain meds McMath prescribed?"

"I'll do it." She started to move past him, but he put a hand on both of her arms, gently holding her in place.

"You can, but I'll just end up following you to the kitchen to make sure you don't need help with the medicine bottle. Then I'll probably walk you back here. Make sure you're okay. In the end we'll waste more time than we need to."

"Are you always so annoyingly reasonable?"

He laughed, released his hold on her arms. "Only with you. Give me two minutes."

He was back in less. A white pill in one hand, a bottle of water in the other. "Here you go. I'm going to get back to work on that back lock. If your brother finishes the front door first, I'll never hear the end of it."

He was gone before she could thank him, pulling the door shut as he left.

Piper popped the pill into her mouth, swallowed it down with water, and glanced around the room. Rest might be what she needed, but the thought of closing her eyes wasn't appealing. Too many nightmares waited to pounce. Work was a better idea.

Her briefcase was sitting on the floor and she pulled out the files she'd picked up in Richmond. She opened the first, tried to read some of the information, but the words were blurry, her mind foggy from lack of sleep. "Okay. I'll go through these tomorrow during my break."

She slid everything back in her briefcase, and grabbed the phone from the bedside table. Much as she'd rather avoid the conversation, she needed to call Wayne, find out why he'd cut her off when she'd tried to ask about the missing antiques.

She dialed his number, listened as the answering machine picked up, and left a message that was brief and to the point. "Wayne. We need to talk about Uncle Marcus's antiques. If you have answers give me a call. If you don't, give me a call."

Now what? She called Miriam. Confirmed their Wednesday meeting. Then pulled the day planner from her briefcase to check the following day's schedule, paced the room, stared out the window and finally collapsed onto the bed. So, this was what it was like to have nothing to do.

She didn't think she liked it.

At least the pain she'd been feeling had eased, the knifelike edge of it replaced by a dull throb. She leaned back against the pillows, relaxing muscles she hadn't realized were tense.

Footsteps sounded in the hall, the refrigerator door opened and shut, ice clinked against glass. Someone must be getting a drink. Piper should get up, offer the men some coffee. Maybe bake some cookies they could all enjoy when they finished their tasks, but her body felt leaden, the effort to move too much, and she let her eyes drift closed...

He was there. Standing outside her window. Black-masked face pressing against the glass. She tried to move, but her muscles refused to respond. And so she lay helpless, watching as he lifted his arm. Held it up. A snake wreathed around his forearm. Not a tattoo. A real one. He pulled it off, slammed its thick, scaly head against the window, laughing as the glass shattered onto the floor of Piper's room. She tried again to move, thrashing against a cocoon that wouldn't release her.

And he was coming in. Sliding through the window, silent now. Intent. One step closer to the bed. Then another. Reaching for the mask, pulling it off his head. But not a human head. A snake's head. His mouth gaped open, huge fangs glistening with poison as he leaned over Piper.

She screamed, jerked upright, heart crashing against her ribs, breath heaving out.

The door to her room banged open, a dark figure raced in.

Piper screamed again. Shoving aside the comforter that imprisoned her, grabbing the crutch from the floor, coming up swinging.

"Whoa!" Cade's voice registered through her panic as he caught hold of the crutch and yanked it from her hand, his eyes hard, cold steel as he tossed it onto the bed and swung around to survey the room. "What happened? What's wrong?"

She wanted to answer, but her throat was dry with remembered fear, her heart still beating erratically.

"Everything okay?" Sean stepped into the room, a butcher knife clutched in his hand.

"I don't know." Cade leaned close, peering into Piper's eyes, one calloused palm gentle against her cheek. "Piper?"

The warmth of his touch seemed to ease the tension that held her mute. She cleared her throat, wiped a shaky hand against her sweats. "I'm okay."

"Your scream didn't sound like you were okay." Cade continued to study her expression as his hand dropped to her shoulder.

"I had a nightmare."

"Must have been a doozy." Sean stepped closer, the knife still clutched in his hand, curiosity in his eyes.

He wanted to know the details, but Piper wasn't up to sharing them. "It was. Where's my brother? Getting a more deadly weapon than the butcher knife?"

Cade's lip quirked, and he shook his head. "I guess the nightmare didn't hurt your sense of humor. Grayson's at the store picking up stuff for the dog. Then he and a friend are going to pick up a car for you."

"A rental?"

"He said something about a station wagon."

"Please tell me you're kidding."

"I'm afraid not."

"Nothing wrong with station wagons. I drove one years ago." Sean broke in, his leg dragging a little as he made his way back out to the hall. "I'm going to brew some coffee. A little pick-me-up will do us all a world of good."

Piper waited until he was out of sight, then turned back to Cade. "I still can't believe Gray is bringing the station wagon here."

"What's wrong with it?"

"Besides the fact that it's a boat?"

"A boat?"

"You remember it. I know you do. It's the same car you and Seth used to drive me to piano in."

His brow furrowed. Then cleared. "That cream-colored monstrosity with the faux wood paneling?"

"That's the one."

"Your parents still have that car? It must have been fifteen years old when Seth was driving it."

"It was. Now it's vintage. Or so my Dad would like us to believe. He says he's going to keep it until his grandkids are past the learning to drive stage. Since he doesn't have any grandkids, that could be a while."

"Knowing your dad, he'll somehow manage to keep it running."

"You're probably right. Though I almost hope the car dies a quick and painless death so Dad will stop handing it off to me every time my car is in the shop."

"I won't tell him you said that. I know how your dad is about his cars."

"How we *both* are about cars. Which is why I want my GTO. Not a '70s boat." She smiled, knowing her impounded car was the least of her worries.

"Jake's being careful. He doesn't want to miss any evidence."

"It's okay. A few days without my car won't kill me."

Other things could. Like that guy she'd dreamed about. But she wouldn't think about that now. "Did Gray say when he'd be back?"

"He shouldn't be long." Cade's deep green eyes followed her movements as she straightened the covers on her bed.

His intensity was unsettling and her cheeks heated as she turned to face him once again. "What?"

"I'm just wishing I had my camera."

"So you could get a picture of me at my worst?"

"So I could capture the strength and vulnerability I see in your face. It would be quite a portrait."

She laughed, the sound hollow and nervous. "Sure it would."

"You don't believe me?" He stepped close, easing behind her and putting his hands on her shoulders. Then turning her so she faced the mirror above her dresser. "Look."

She did. And saw a woman with flyaway strands of straight blond hair, pale cheeks stained pink, worry and fear turning her gray eyes to slate. She lifted a hand to smooth her hair, embarrassed and not sure why. Cade had known her during the awkward years. The years of skinny arms and pointy elbows. The frizzy perm that made her hair fall out. Makeup experiments gone wrong. He'd watched all of it along with her brothers. Even laughed. So why should she care that he was seeing her like this now?

She wasn't sure she wanted to know the answer to that, and turned from the mirror and from Cade. "Like I said, 'sure, it would.'"

"I guess beauty is in the eye of the beholder." His words were light. "Come on. Let's go see what my father is up to." He put a hand on her elbow, the rough calluses on his hands rasping against her skin as he led her from the room.

Sean was waiting in the kitchen, eager to talk about Piper's music, her job, the book she was writing, the dog that would arrive the next day. She answered his questions, did her best to act engaged, enthusiastic and eager to chat. But her mind kept returning to Cade's words. *Beauty is in the eye of the beholder.*

Did that mean he found beauty in her? More importantly, did she want him to?

Piper wasn't sure. She only knew that her life was too complicated, too busy to be wasting so much time thinking about a man. Especially since she'd already decided she didn't want or need another one in her life.

And she'd been right. Hadn't she? Or had the decision been a knee-jerk reaction to too many disappointments, too many men who'd fallen short of the mark?

She didn't know. But she cared. And that surprised Piper almost as much as Cade's words had.

FIFTEEN

She drove the station wagon, aka the boat to work the next day. Despite its size and age it purred like a kitten and handled beautifully. If she ignored the exterior, she had to admit it was almost as nice a ride as the GTO. Parking it wasn't nearly as pleasant. She managed to squeeze in between an oversize SUV and a tiny compact, grabbed her crutch, briefcase and purse from the seat, and headed to class. Her last class of the summer. She couldn't ever remember being so relieved to be finishing up a semester. A few people called out to her as she made her way through the bustling corridor. She waved, smiled and kept going.

She wasn't up to idle chitchat, didn't feel like explaining why she was using a crutch or how she'd been injured. All she wanted to do was administer the exam so she could track Wayne down. He hadn't returned her call and she wasn't sure he still planned to meet with her. That bothered Piper. A lot. He knew how important the exhibit was to her, how pleased Marcus would have been to know its grand opening would coincide with Music Makers' twenty-fifth anniversary. Wayne knew, yet he'd been putting her off and making excuses for weeks. Why? It had to be more than a busy schedule and a stressful life.

Or was it? Maybe all the talk of Wayne's financial difficulties was making her see intrigue where none existed.

One way or another, Piper wanted answers and she had every intention of getting them. Today. If Wayne stood her up, she'd go to Music Makers and confront him there.

By the time she'd collected the last of the teacher evaluation sheets and said goodbye to her students, Piper knew Wayne wasn't coming. She shoved the exams into her briefcase, grabbed her cell phone. There were three messages. Not one of them was from Wayne. She dialed Grayson's number first.

"Sinclair."

"Hey, Grayson. It's me. I got your message. What's up?"

"I'm free for lunch in an hour. Want to meet me?"

"I wish I could. The home visit is this afternoon and I want to get everything set up for Samson."

"You think the dog's going to care if his food and water aren't set out when he arrives?" There was a note of amusement in his voice. Piper ignored it.

"I think the SPCA might."

"Good point. How's your day going?"

"Besides the fact that Wayne stood me up, great."

"I didn't know you were meeting Wayne." Grayson's voice had taken on the quiet calm he used when he was upset.

"Because it isn't a big deal. He's supposed to be coming to the college to discuss Marcus's antique collection."

"You're not planning on going anywhere with him?"

"Would it matter if I was?"

"He's a suspect, Piper."

"He's also family. If you were the one the police suspected, I'd still get together with you, still talk to you. How can I treat Wayne any differently?"

"Easy. Just say 'no, I can't meet with you.'"

"You're being purposely obtuse."

"I'm being purposely cautious. It's your life we're talking about. You can't afford to take any chances."

"And I won't."

He sighed. "This conversation is going nowhere fast and I've got a meeting in two minutes. Be careful, Piper. I'll see you tonight."

He hung up before she had a chance to say goodbye, and Piper slid the cell phone back into her briefcase. She'd return the other two calls later.

The hall reverberated with chatter and laughter as students hurried from one class to another. Piper joined the throng, the crutch awkward and ungainly as she tried to maneuver through the crowded hallway. The staircase was even worse, people hurrying past, nearly tripping over her as they rushed along.

"Piper! Hold up."

Wayne. She turned, relief easing some of her tension. He hadn't stood her up after all. Which meant he wasn't guilty of anything. She hoped. "I thought you weren't coming."

"I got held up at a meeting at work."

"Anything exciting?"

"Just John's bimonthly pep rally. Two hours discussing all the good Music Makers is doing."

"You sound less than peppy."

"I love Music Makers, Piper. You know that. But sitting in meetings discussing how wonderful the foundation is, is a waste of my time."

"I can understand that. I'm not much for meetings, either. So, what did you want to talk to me about?"

"Not much. I wanted to touch base, make sure you were okay."

"I am."

He nodded, his gaze drifting away from Piper, and touching on the stairs, the people passing them. "We're blocking traffic. How about I walk you outside?"

"All right."

"Hand me your briefcase. I'll carry it for you."

She hesitated, Grayson's words spinning through her mind. Was handing Wayne her briefcase, walking outside with him, taking chances? Her heart said no. Her head wasn't so sure.

She went with her heart, thrusting the briefcase

toward him with a smile that must have looked as forced as it felt. "Thanks. Getting down the stairs on one crutch isn't easy. That briefcase was making it downright treacherous."

"No problem. Where are you parked?"

"The faculty lot."

"Really? I was looking for your GTO and didn't see it."

"That's because I've got Dad's Chevy."

"Not the boat?"

"I'm afraid so."

"So the GTO is out of commission."

"Unfortunately, yes."

"What's wrong this time? Transmission?"

"Evidence."

"Say again?"

"Jake's going over the car with a fine-tooth comb, searching for evidence. When he's finished, I'll have my car back. And it can't happen too soon."

Wayne had gone silent, his eyes shuttered behind his glasses.

"Wayne?"

He shook his head, smiled. "Sorry. What kind of evidence did you say he was looking for?"

"I didn't. I was just told evidence."

"That doesn't seem odd to you?"

"Should it?"

"I think so. You were shot. The person who did it was in a car a few thousand feet away. How much evidence could there be on your GTO?"

"They found a nail in the tire. Shiny and brand-new. Maybe they're hoping to find something else."

"Or maybe they know something you don't."

"Like?"

"Wish I knew." He pushed the door to the stairwell open, and gestured Piper out into bright sunlight. "Not that it matters. The composite the media showcased last night was amazing."

"I didn't see it." She'd fallen asleep after Cade left, only to wake up at eleven, restless and unable to sleep.

"Anyone who's ever seen the tattoo will recognize it. The fact that the police are offering a two-thousand-dollar reward is a lot of incentive for someone to come forward."

"Two thousand dollars? That's it? I thought I was worth much more than that." She meant it as a joke. Wayne didn't seem to find it amusing. His already dark expression becoming darker.

"You are." He spoke quietly, but Piper heard the words above the hubbub of courtyard activities.

"Thanks."

He didn't respond, just led the way through the courtyard, his silence oppressive.

Piper kept pace beside him, struggling with the crutch and her own awkward movements. "So, when are you going to tell me?"

He glanced over, obviously startled. "Tell you what?"

"The real reason you came today. If you'd just wanted to make sure I was okay you could have called."

"You're right." He stopped where he was, turning to face Piper. "I do have something to tell you, but it's not easy."

"It will be once you share it."

He smiled, brushed Piper's hair away from her forehead. "If there were more people like you, the world would be a better place."

"Stop trying to butter me up and spill."

"I sold the coronet, the Beatles record and the sheet music."

"*You* sold them?" She said it more to herself than to him, but he nodded anyway.

"At the time I wasn't thinking of who they'd go to once Marcus died. All I knew was that we needed money. Marcus wanted another trip to Mexico, another chance at a miracle cure, but we didn't have the cash. I took the coronet and sold it to a friend of his. A few months later when Marcus went on another cure jag, I sold the other two items."

"Did he know?"

"No. He already felt like a burden. Telling him about our financial difficulties would have only made things worse for him."

"But he would have wanted to know."

"Would he? He was dying, Piper, he knew it. I knew it. What good would it have done to tell him how much of a financial drain his illness had become?"

"But—"

"Would you have done things differently? Made a better choice?"

Would she have? She couldn't answer the question. Didn't even dare try. "I don't know."

He watched her for a moment, his eyes dark behind his glasses, his expression unreadable. "That's something, anyway. I wondered if you'd say you would have, that you would have known right away that telling him was the right thing to do. For me it wasn't so cut-and-dry."

"I can understand that. You made a tough choice. You did it for Marcus. What I don't understand, what I can't understand, is why you've been lying about it." There. It was out. Her disappointment obvious, she knew, in the words and in her face. She'd trusted him. He hadn't been nearly as sure of her.

"Think about it, Piper. Marcus was a financial burden. I can't deny it. All the love in the world, all feelings of obligation in the world couldn't change that. When he died I was out of town. A convenient coincidence, don't you think?"

"I hadn't really thought about it." Not until yesterday. Since then, she'd been thinking of little else.

"What's sad is that you probably haven't. It would never occur to you to question Marcus's death because it would never occur to you that someone could be desperate enough to murder an invalid." There was a harshness to his voice Piper didn't like, a snideness that set her teeth on edge.

"Your point is?"

"My point is that other people aren't as unjaded as you. When I found out Marcus was dead, found out how he had died, I knew I would be under suspicion. I was sure the police would dig into my financial status, see how desperate things were, and draw some erroneous conclusions. When they didn't, I was relieved and ready to put it all behind me."

"Until the will was read and you found out that I was inheriting the collection."

"Marcus had never said anything about the collection. He'd told me I was inheriting the house. I assumed that meant everything in it. I was wrong. Of course, by the time I found out it was too late."

"You should have told me."

"I meant to, but every time I tried the words seemed inadequate. I stole from a man who loved me, who'd given me my entire life back. How could I justify that?"

"Wayne—"

"You can't understand, Piper. No matter how hard you try. If it had been you, you would have done the right thing—admitted to selling the antiques, apologized, probably worked out a payment plan and gotten a second job."

"I—"

"But it was me—a man with a history of theft and gambling, a man who's already proven he isn't trustworthy. How could I face your family, how could I face you, after I admitted I'd done it again—stole again, spent the money again? Lied again." His voice shook, emotion bleeding through every word, and Piper's heart clenched.

"Not my family, Wayne. *Our* family. And you did it for a good reason. I understand that."

His jaw hardened and he turned away, his words coming fast and soft. "I need a few days. Just a few. Then I'll be ready to go to the police, tell them what I did. Can you give me that?"

Could she? They were at the crosswalk, the light flashing for them to move. Wayne stepped out with the crowd, hurrying across the busy intersection. It took Piper a moment longer to step off the curb and into the street. She wanted to hurry after Wayne, tell him everything was going to be okay, but he was already pulling ahead, putting distance between them.

Piper's focus was on Wayne. Maybe that was why she wasn't prepared for what happened next.

One minute she was hobbling along in the crosswalk, cars whizzing by to her left as they entered the college campus, the next someone shoved into her from behind. She screamed, the crutch flying, her body tilting. Another shove and she didn't have the breath to scream. She was falling, could hear a horn blare, feel pavement skidding under her hands. She braced herself for impact, knowing there was nothing she could do, no way she could stop what was about to happen.

SIXTEEN

"Are you okay?" Feet slammed against pavement, a hand reached for Piper's.

Piper grabbed it, looking up into the misty green eyes of a woman she didn't know.

"I think so." She let herself be pulled upright, her gaze scanning the area, her heart beating triple-time.

A sporty red car idled less than a foot away, the driver's door open. Several people stood nearby, wide-eyed, shocked and seemingly as shaken as Piper felt.

"Piper!" Wayne raced into the street, his glasses sliding down his nose, his eyes wide with fear. "What happened?"

"I don't know. I—"

"Some jerk was in too big a hurry and shoved into her. Like he couldn't see she was on a crutch. I nearly ran her over." The woman's voice was shaking, her hands visibly trembling as she grabbed the crutch and handed it to Piper. "Are you sure you're okay?"

"Yes. I'm sure." But her heart was beating too

fast, the world spinning around her, fading from bright to dim, gray to black. She blinked, trying to pull herself together.

"You look like a ghost. Come on. Over here." Wayne lifted her, carrying her the rest of the way across the street and setting her down in the grass. "Head between your knees. Take a few deep breaths."

She did, listening to the ebb and flow of voices around her. The high-pitched sound of other people's excitement and fear.

"Better?" Wayne watched her, his eyes clouded with rage.

"Yes. Thanks."

"Good. Stay here. I'm going to find the guy that did this." He stood, leaving Piper's briefcase at her side, his gaze scanning the small throng of people who watched.

"You won't. Find him, I mean." The woman knelt beside Piper, but her gaze was on Wayne. "He waited to see what happened, then took off running."

Piper met Wayne's eyes and knew he was thinking the same thing she was. "Maybe we'd better call the police."

He nodded, lifted his cell phone and dialed.

"How about a smile this time, guys?" Cade raised his camera and snapped a quick shot of the four teenagers who'd just won a local spelling bee. They obliged, lifting trophies and medals, hamming it up for the camera. An easy shot—four happy, healthy kids. These were the kinds of photos that took little thought or preparation. The kind Cade enjoyed for the simple relaxation of it.

"Good. We're done."

"Thanks again for doing this, Cade." Sandy leaned back in her chair, one hand on her protruding stomach, the notepad she'd been using to write down names and ages in the other.

"No need to thank me for doing my job." He lifted the camera, snapped a shot of her blossoming with new life, soft in a way she hadn't been before her pregnancy.

"Hey! Next time warn me. I don't even have makeup on."

"You don't need it. You look great. Jim is going to love these pictures. So are you." He snapped another picture, and dodged her hand as she lunged up and tried to grab the camera. "None of that. You go into early labor because I took a few pictures and Jim will have my head."

"And I'll have your head if you show up in the delivery room with that camera."

"No way. I'm sending it in with Jim. But I'll be there afterwards to take a million shots of you and the little one." He took one more shot, catching her look of exasperated affection.

"Do you have to head back to Lakeview now? Or do you want to grab some lunch somewhere?"

"Lunch sounds good." He'd left home too early to eat breakfast, and the half pack of crackers he'd devoured since then had done little to fill him.

Though he hadn't pulled a shift last night, he'd gone to the station, working with Jake late into the night, tracing down leads that had come in after the composite sketch aired. So far every lead had been a dead end.

"You look tired, Cade. Is everything okay?"

"Just working on a case. It's a tough one."

"Want to talk about it? I promise I won't breathe a word."

Cade's cell phone rang, saving him the need to gently decline. He glanced at the number. Jake. This could be good or bad news. He was praying it was the first, that Jake had finally gotten a lead that panned out. "Macalister here."

"Where are you?"

Jake's tone put Cade on high alert, and he straightened, shifting his camera bag over his shoulder. "Lynchburg."

"How close to the university?"

"Maybe ten minutes."

"We've got trouble there. I'm on my way. I need you there ten minutes ago."

"I'm on it." He knew without asking that Piper was part of the trouble, and mouthed an apology at Sandy as he jogged from the room with the phone still pressed to his ear. "What happened?"

"Piper was shoved in front of a car."

Everything inside Cade went cold. "How bad is she?"

"Car missed her by less than a foot."

"Witnesses?"

"Only one who saw how everything played out. Lynchburg PD is taking statements. It's their gig. They've invited us in on it because we're working the case in Lakeview."

"In other words, don't step on any toes."

"You got it. I'll see you ASAP."

It took ten minutes to drive to Lynchburg University. It seemed like a lifetime. Three police cruisers were parked in the faculty parking lot. Cade pulled in beside them, his eyes scanning the crowd that huddled on the sidewalk. No one stood out. Each face reflected curiosity, worry, fear. None looked guilty. But then, he hadn't expected the perpetrator to stick around. Not this time. There was too much at stake. Too many people looking for him.

"Are you from the Lakeview Sheriff's Department?" A fresh-faced officer with a bad case of acne stepped up close to Cade.

"Yes." He flashed his badge.

"We've got Ms. Sinclair in our cruiser. This way."

She huddled in the front seat of the car, pale, shaken, a briefcase in her lap, the crutch clutched in her hand.

He gestured to it, forcing lightness to his voice that he didn't feel. "Are you planning to take a swing at me?"

"My hands are shaking too hard to lift it." Her voice wobbled, and she blinked hard. Not tears. Not from Piper. Cade could count on one hand the number of times he'd seen her cry when she was a kid.

"Hey. It's going to be okay."

"No thanks to the guy who pushed her." Wayne spoke from the seat next to Piper, his thick hair standing on end, his expression grim. "A half a foot closer and she'd be dead."

"It wasn't that close, Wayne."

"Close enough to be too close for comfort."

"Don't remind me." Piper shivered, rubbing her hands up and down her arms, wincing a little with the movement. There were scrapes on her knuckles and on the palms of her hands. Her unbandaged knee, peeking out from beneath her skirt, was raw and weeping.

Cade reached out to brush a finger along a pale pink scratch on her cheek. "You really took a beating."

"Not too bad, but I think my shoulder is bleeding."

"Let's see."

She shifted, wincing again, and revealing a deep red stain on the satiny fabric of her tank top.

"Mind if I look?"

"Go ahead."

Cade eased the strap of her tank down just enough to peel back the bandage that covered her bullet wound. "You opened up the wound again. We'll need to get it restitched."

"Great." Her voice cracked, and this time there was no mistaking the tears in her eyes.

"Come here." He tugged at her hand, urging her up out of the car, ignoring the thud of her briefcase as it fell to the pavement. She was warm and pliant in his arms, her head resting against his chest. That was almost as worrisome as her tears.

Cade met Wayne's eyes. There was something there—guilt, anger. Now wasn't the time to think about it. Later he'd decide what it all meant. "Did you call her brother?"

"He's on his way."

"Can you call him again? Tell him to meet us at the hospital?"

"No." Piper shoved away from Cade's chest, sniffing back tears she could barely contain. "I can't go to the hospital, yet. I've got to get home."

"You've got to get stitched up again. Anything else can wait." Cade's voice was rough with worry or with anger.

"Samson can't." But he was right. Her shoulder hurt. More than she wanted to say.

"The dog? I can take care of that for you." Wayne stepped out of the cruiser. Did Cade sense his tension? Piper thought so, as he was watching Wayne with the unwavering stare of a predator ready to pounce.

When Cade spoke, his voice had changed, gone cold and sharp-edged. "That's your brother's car pulling up. Give me the key to your house and I'll take care of getting Samson settled."

"I can't ask you to do that."

"You didn't ask. I'm offering. Keys?"

Piper hesitated. The thought of Wayne going to her house, using the key to get in, hanging out there alone, hadn't bothered her. When she thought about Cade doing the same it seemed too intimate, too…

What? How could it possibly be any different just because Cade was doing it? It couldn't. It would be one friend helping another. Nothing more or less than that.

She told herself that as she fished her keys out of the front pocket of her briefcase and handed them to him. "Okay. Thanks. Grayson put the dog crate in my office. I was thinking it should be in the kitchen. I want to get Samson's bowls out, too. And pour him a little food." She was rambling, knew it, and was helpless to stop the flow of words. "That bed Grayson picked up? It can go on the floor in the living room. Maybe—"

"I'll handle it."

"But—"

"Stop worrying."

"I can't. It's a natural part of who I am."

"I know. I can remember you pestering Seth about one thing after another. You used to drive us both crazy."

"And still do, I'm sure."

"Piper!" Grayson hurried over, his hair ruffled, his tie crooked. "I can't believe this." His eyes flashed with fury, but his hand was gentle as he grabbed hers. "Are you okay? You're bleeding." He lifted the bandage on her shoulder, just as Cade had, and surveyed the wound. "This needs to be cleaned up and stitched again."

He stepped away, his gaze hardening when he spotted Wayne. "You were here. Tell me how this happened."

"Someone shoved Piper out into traffic."

"And you didn't try to stop him?"

"Gray—" Piper started.

"I was in front of her in the crosswalk. I didn't even see the guy coming."

"You were in *front* of her. Why not beside her? Didn't it occur to you that she might be in danger?" Gray's fury spilled out in cutting sarcasm.

"That's enough, Gray." Cade's voice brooked no argument, and Grayson had the decency to flush.

"Right. Sorry. I'm upset. It's probably better if I take Piper to the hospital and leave you to do your job, Cade."

They exchanged a look, and Piper was sure Wayne would be given the third degree after she left. Was that good or bad? Would he tell them what he'd told her? Should she? The questions raced through her mind as Grayson led her to his car and helped her inside.

In the end she kept silent, wanting to give Wayne an opportunity to face the police and tell the truth. She could only pray she wouldn't live to regret it.

The sun had already hit its zenith and started toward the horizon by the time the emergency room physician restitched Piper's wound. Sore, tired and still shaken from her near miss, she sat in Grayson's car, watching the trees whiz by as he drove her home.

"You're quiet." He spoke softly as if afraid of spooking her.

There was a question in the words, and Piper

brushed at the hem of her skirt, trying to decide what to tell him. "Just tired, I guess."

"It's been a long few days."

"Yeah." Should she tell him about Wayne and the antiques? If she did, what would happen? Would they arrest Wayne? Would things be easier for Wayne if he confessed what he'd done himself?

She didn't know. Couldn't know.

"Piper?"

"What?" She blinked, caught Grayson's concerned look.

"I asked if you wanted me to stop at the Dairy Queen before we go back to your place."

"Are you hungry?"

"I grabbed something while they were stitching you up."

"Then, no."

"How about the diner? I can grab you one of Doris's pot pies and a brownie sundae for dessert."

"I'm not hungry."

"You still need to eat."

"I'll grab something at home."

"Look, if you fade away Mom won't be happy. Let's—"

"Grayson, I really want to go home. Cade's there with Samson and I don't want him to have to puppy-sit for too long." A partial truth. Anything else would have to wait until she spoke to Wayne again.

The bungalow's lights glowed a warm welcome as Grayson pulled into Piper's driveway. She maneuvered out of the car, grabbing her briefcase from the seat beside her.

"Let me." Grayson took it from her, put a hand beneath her elbow. "You finally get to welcome your new housemate. Excited?"

It was a deliberate bid to pull her out of her silence, and Piper tried to smile, tried to sound enthusiastic. "More like terrified."

"It'll work out."

"I hope so." She pushed the door open, heard a low bark and nearly fell backward as Samson slid across the wood floor and slammed into her.

"I said no, mutt!" Cade grabbed Samson by the collar and pulled him back, but not before a rough, wet tongue scraped across Piper's face.

She laughed, swiping the moisture off with the back of her hand and leaning down to scratch Samson behind his ears, some of her anxiety fading away in the face of the dog's exuberance. "I guess the house passed inspection."

"With flying colors."

"Good. At least that's one thing that's gone right." The words slipped out before she could stop them, and she hated the self-pity she heard in them. She straightened, pasted on a smile. "I really appreciate you doing this for me, Cade. You've gone above and beyond the call of duty."

"Who said anything about duty? This was about friendship."

"Then I appreciate it even more." So why did she

sound so lackluster, so ungrateful. "Has Samson eaten anything?"

"A better question would be—is there anything he hasn't eaten? I ordered a pizza, put it on the kitchen table, turned my back for two minutes and it was gone."

"Samson! How could you? And after Cade has been so good to you."

To his credit, the dog looked repentant, his head down, his eyes sad.

"He's got that 'I'm a good dog who had a bad moment' look down pat. No wonder you wanted to bring him home." Grayson reached down to pat the dog's head.

Samson collapsed in a heap on the floor, rolling onto his back, his tongue lolling in ecstasy as Grayson scratched his belly.

Piper stepped around them both, feeling shaky and tired.

"You're pale. Are you in pain?" Cade leaned a shoulder against the wall as he spoke.

"Are you kidding? They shot me up with enough painkiller to keep me numb for a week."

"Hungry? I ordered a whole new pizza. Samson didn't manage to grab any of it."

"No. Just tired. If you guys don't mind, I think I'll lie down for a while."

Grayson's hand froze on Samson's belly, his gray eyes dark and filled with worry. "Go ahead. I've got a dinner meeting tonight, but I'll cancel it."

"No. Don't. I'm fine. A quick nap and I'll be even

better." She hurried away, blinking back more of the tears she'd been fighting for hours.

When had life gotten so completely out of her control? How was it possible she hadn't seen the truth about the antiques before now? Had Wayne confessed to the police yet? Piper couldn't ask Cade. Not without garnering a whole lot of suspicion.

She swung the door closed, jumping back in surprise when it flew open once again. Samson stood at the threshold, tail wagging, big doggy grin begging her to let him come in. "Come on, then."

He settled on the throw rug near the bed.

Piper pulled on a pair of sweats and an oversize T-shirt and lay down on top of the comforter, her mind racing with one worry after another, one question after another. She needed answers, but didn't know where to turn to find them. "God, please, please tell me what I should do."

There was no answer. Just the sound of her own heartbeat and the raspy huff of Sampson's breath.

SEVENTEEN

Piper paced from one end of her room to the other. Watching the clock. Two in the morning. Again. Wishing Grayson were back. He'd called at ten, said there was a crisis and that he'd be there as soon as it was resolved.

Apparently it still wasn't resolved, and Piper was alone in the house, darkness pressing against the windows, danger waiting for an opportunity to find her again.

As if sensing her fear, Samson huffed, nosed his head under Piper's hand. "Okay. So I'm not quite alone."

She grabbed her crutch and left her bedroom, turning on the lights in the hall, the bathroom, the living room and the kitchen. The morning room she left dark, easing down onto the piano bench, every muscle in her body protesting.

"What do you think, Samson? A hymn? Or something more contemporary?"

Her fingers moved over the keys, finding the melody

that drifted through her mind. "'Melancholie.' I hope you don't mind sad." The haunting tune filled the room, the tempo rising and falling with each turn of phrase. She hit the crescendo, eased back on the repeat, letting the music take her away from her worries, letting herself get lost in the song, so caught up in the movement Samson's first bark barely registered.

He barked again, a loud, deep warning, and Piper's fingers tripped, stumbled to a stop.

"What is it, boy?"

He growled, low, mean, and paced into the living room, the scruff of his neck standing on end.

Piper's heart slammed in her chest, and she followed him to the front window. He nosed aside the curtain, his massive head disappearing behind its thick folds as he continued to bark.

"Hush. Everything's okay." She hoped.

Piper put a hand on the dog's back, felt the tension in his muscles. What did he see? What did he sense? Was someone outside? Piper wanted to run back to her room and pull the covers over her head, pretend nothing was wrong.

But she couldn't. Nor could she call 911 without first checking to be sure Samson wasn't barking at a deer, a cat, or one of her neighbors coming home from a very late night. She reached for the curtain, imagined pulling it back, seeing the masked figure from her dream. Imagined the snake flying through the window, fangs exposed, ready to kill.

Her heart crashed against her ribs, her stomach

twisted into knots, but she eased the curtains back anyway, and peered out into darkness. Shadows drifted across the yard, sinister shapes that could have been anything or nothing at all. Piper blinked, trying to adjust her eyes, saw a car parked at the curb in front of her house. Was someone in it? She thought she saw movement. Imagined a bullet shattering the glass, and let the curtains drop.

Paranoid or not, she was calling for help.

She grabbed the phone, her fingers trembling, her entire body shaking with fear. The phone rang before she could dial, and she dropped it, fumbling to pick it up again, to answer.

"Hello?"

"What are you doing up at two in the morning?" Cade's voice drifted across the line, a little rough, a little raspy, and such a relief Piper almost sagged to the floor.

"Listening to Samson bark. Someone's parked in front of my house." Did she sound as scared as she felt? Probably.

"That would be me."

"You?" She wasn't quite sure she'd heard correctly, couldn't imagine what Cade would be doing outside her house at two in the morning. She walked over to the window, pulled the shades open, watching as the interior light went on in the car.

A police cruiser. She could see that now. Just as she could see the shape of the man sitting in the driver's seat, see his quick wave.

She waved back, smiling despite herself. "What are you doing out here?"

"I'm on patrol. I've been down this street ten times tonight."

"Really?"

"Jake's orders. Of course, I'd be doing it anyway. Orders or not."

"I wish I'd known."

"Why's that?"

"It might have saved me another sleepless night."

"There's still time to get some sleep. Go get in bed. I'll stay here for a while."

"I still won't sleep. Every time I close my eyes I see violence—guns, snakes, attackers lying in wait."

"More nightmares?" His voice was warm honey, tempting her to tell him everything.

"My imagination working overtime."

"A few more days and this will all be over."

"I hope so." Did she sound as pitiful as she felt? She cleared her throat, trying to put more energy and life into her voice. "I've got too many things to do to keep getting sidetracked."

"Getting sidetracked isn't always a bad thing. Even you need to take a break once in a while."

"I take breaks."

"Do you?"

"Of course." Though, if pressed, she wasn't sure she could name a recent vacation.

"That's not what I hear."

"What do you hear?"

"That you're constantly working—teaching college, private piano lessons, playing piano at church. You've got a book to put together—"

"Everyone has to make a living, Cade." She cut him off, the list of her duties doing nothing to ease her anxiety. "Those jobs are my livelihood."

"Are they? So how much are you getting paid to write the Music Makers book?"

"I'm doing it as a favor to Miriam and as a memorial to my uncle. I don't want to get paid for it."

"And helping get the exhibit set up?"

"Same thing."

"And the fund-raiser?"

"Is there a point to this?"

"Just asking."

"I'm not getting paid anything. I don't want to get paid anything. I'm doing this for my uncle. For Music Makers. For all the kids out there who want to learn to play an instrument, but whose parents don't have the money to make that possible."

"And that's why half your piano students are on scholarship."

"How do you know that? My own family doesn't know it."

"People talk, Piper. They say good things, or bad things, depending on the person they're talking about. When you're a police officer investigating a case, you hear it all. People like you. They respect you. They worry about you. They say you do too much for too many people and not nearly enough for yourself."

"They don't need to worry. I'm fine." But her throat was tight, tears she'd been holding back sliding down her cheeks. She let the curtain fall back into place, dropped onto the couch.

"You still there?"

"Where would I go?"

"I've upset you. I'm sorry."

"No. You haven't. I was already upset."

"Tell me."

"There's nothing to say that you don't already know. My life was going along just fine. Now it's spinning out of control and I don't know how to stop it."

"Maybe you can't."

"Thanks. That's comforting." She rubbed a tear from her cheek, stared up at the ceiling.

"Maybe *you* can't. God can. And He will. We've got some more leads to follow. More information coming in."

"Like what?"

"Let's make a deal. You go lay down for a few hours. I'm off duty at eight. I'll stop by then. Tell you what I know."

"Tell me now."

"And miss an opportunity to get slobbered on by your dog? I don't think so. Get some rest, Piper. I'll see you soon." There was a quiet click, then the hum of the dial tone.

The phone rang before the sun came up, waking Piper from a restless sleep. She winced, reaching for the phone that sat on the end table, and wishing she'd slept in her bed instead of on the couch. "Hello?"

"Piper, it's Wayne. Did I wake you?"

"Sort of." She glanced at her watch, barely stifled a groan when she saw the time. "It's five-thirty."

"I know. I'm getting ready for work. I wanted to call and see how you were doing."

"I'm worried. Did you talk to the police? Tell them about the antiques?"

"Not yet. Listen, Piper, I have a big favor to ask you."

Uh-oh. This didn't sound good. "What favor?"

"I was looking through my records, trying to find the receipts for Marcus's treatments. They're gone."

"Gone? How can that be?"

"I don't know. Things have been so hectic this past year. I'm not even sure I filed them. Without those receipts I can't prove I used the money from the sale of the antiques to fund Marcus's treatments." He fell silent and Piper could imagine him raking a hand through his hair and pushing his glasses up.

"So go to the police. Tell them what you told me. They'll help you get everything you need."

"They'll book me and lock me up. Then they'll check out my story."

"You don't know that, Wayne. I'm sure they'll be—"

"Piper, can you think of one other person who has as much to gain as I do if you die? Just one?"

She went cold at his words, not wanting to face the truth. "No."

"And neither can the police. They've been asking questions for days. Talking to my friends. My co-workers. Checking into my background. My finances. I'm their prime suspect. I'm their *only* suspect. When they find out I sold those antiques, when I can't offer proof of what I did with the money, they'll think I'm guilty."

"If you don't have receipts, what about cancelled checks? Credit card statements?"

"They were all cash transactions, Piper. The only proof I've got are those receipts and I don't even have those." His words whipped out, harsh, angry, nothing like what Piper was used to from Wayne.

"There's got to be a way to get copies."

He took a deep breath, as if trying to control his frustration. "I've tried to contact the facility in Mexico. I can't reach anyone there. It's been over a year. Maybe they don't even exist any longer."

"The police."

"I don't need the police. I need time. I know those receipts are here somewhere. Give me until tomorrow night. If I don't find them by then, I'll go to the police myself."

"But—"

"Have you ever been arrested? Ever been finger-printed? Booked?"

"You know I haven't."

"It's a hundred times worse than you can ever

imagine. I don't want to go through it again. Not when I haven't done anything wrong."

"Wayne, I—"

"Just until tomorrow night. That's all the time I'm asking."

"All right." It didn't seem like such a bad thing when Piper agreed, so why did she have a sinking feeling in her stomach as she hung up the phone, and why did the still, quiet voice inside her say that keeping information from the police was exactly what she should *not* be doing?

"What do you think, Samson? Is waiting the wrong thing to do?" The dog sat up, head cocked, tongue lolling.

"Very helpful. Come on, let's get you outside and get me a shower before Cade gets here."

It was a little after eight when Cade pulled up in front of Piper's house. The storybook look of the bungalow was enhanced by golden sunlight filtering through the trees. Cute and tidy, the house seemed to fit Piper's personality and style. The door opened and she stepped out onto the front stoop. Golden hair pulled back into a neat braid, a pair of faded sweatpants sitting low on her waist and a bright orange T-shirt falling against slender curves, she looked young and pretty.

He stepped out of the car, smiling at the picture she made. "You're up. I was hoping you'd be sleeping."

"So you could wake me from all the wonderful dreams I've been having?"

"I would have gone home. Come back later."

"And missed being slobbered on by the dog? Come on in. Samson's going crazy waiting to say hello and I've got a cup of coffee with your name on it."

"Two of the three things I was most looking forward to this morning."

"And the third?" She closed the door, led him into the kitchen.

"Spending some time with you."

She laughed, amusement chasing away the fatigue and worry in her eyes. "That's a load of blarney if I've ever heard it. You must be taking lessons from your father."

"Guilty as charged. I called to check in a few minutes ago and he fed me that line word for word. Even gave me a segue into it."

"I can't believe you actually used it."

"Why not? It served its purpose."

"Which was?"

"To make you laugh."

Her hand stilled, the coffeepot she was lifting freezing in midair. Then she was moving again, pouring the coffee, offering him the cup, a half smile curving her lips. "You're still full of it, Cade Macalister."

"Of what?"

"Whatever made all those high school girls chase after you."

"There weren't that many."

She snorted, grabbed a can of soda from the fridge. "There were scores. Weekly. You'd come over to the house after school and half the cheerleading squad would arrive to *study* with you."

"You remember that?"

"Remember? It was kind of hard to practice piano with a bunch of teenage girls giggling and simpering in the other room. I'd listen to them and think 'no way will I ever act like that over a boy.'"

"Did you?"

"What do you think?" She smiled again.

"I can't see you giggling or simpering."

"I didn't. Except once. But he was a concert pianist. Maybe twenty-one to my fourteen. We met at music camp. He was a guest speaker."

"A summer romance?" His voice was light, though the thought of a twenty-one-year-old paying attention to a fourteen-year-old girl set his teeth on edge.

"Did I say that? You asked if I simpered and giggled. That was my one and only time. Not that it did any good. Anthony didn't know I was alive." She sighed dramatically, settled down into a chair. "So, tell me how the investigation is going." Her skin was pale to the point of translucence, her already slender fingers looking too thin against the can she held. She'd lost weight in the past week, the shadows under her eyes testifying to too many sleepless nights.

"Sure. But first breakfast." He opened the fridge, took out a carton of eggs, an onion, a pepper and cheese.

"What are you doing?"

"Making an omelette. I don't know about you, but I'm starving." He cracked eggs into a bowl, started chopping the onion.

"I hadn't thought about it, but I guess I could eat. Let me do it." She started to rise, and he pressed her back down into the chair.

"Relax. I know my way around the kitchen. The dog been fed yet? He's eyeing me like I'm a slab of raw meat."

"Don't worry. I fed the beast."

"Good. I wouldn't want him to make a meal of me."

"There's no chance of that. Samson's not the kind of dog that likes to work for a meal."

"Who does? Fortunately, an omelette like this isn't much work." Cade slid a plate in front of Piper, and sat down across the table with his own plate.

She speared the eggs with her fork, pushing them around on her plate, but not eating. "We were going to discuss the investigation."

"We've got a good lead on the tattoo. A guy from a mechanic shop in Roanoke said he works with a guy by the name of Paul Martin. Says Martin has a tattoo just like the one that aired on the news."

"That's great!"

"Not as great as it could be. Martin didn't show up for work yesterday. His landlady said he left his apartment late Sunday night and hasn't returned."

"Do you think he saw the news and ran?"

"It's a logical assumption. Time will prove it one

way or another." He polished off his food, eyed Piper's uneaten eggs. "Aren't you going to eat?"

"I guess I'm really not hungry after all. Sorry you wasted the effort."

"It wasn't wasted." He wanted to push her to take a few bites, but Piper knew her own mind. Pushing would only make her sink her heels in.

She stood, put the plate in the sink. "Have you found anything else? Evidence? New suspects?"

"Same suspects. No new evidence, though we're getting close."

"So you have new information on Wayne and Brian?"

"Nothing new on Brian. Wayne's another story. If we had evidence, we'd probably be taking him in for questioning. As it is, we're digging deep. What we're finding isn't flattering."

If they had evidence.

What kind of evidence? The kind that might include antiques taken and sold from Uncle Marcus? Would that be enough for them to bring Wayne in for questioning? And if it was enough, shouldn't Piper tell Cade what she knew?

"Cade, I need to tell you something."

The tone of her voice must have warned him she had something big to share. He straightened, leaned toward her. "Go ahead."

"It's about—"

Cade's cell phone rang. He glanced at the number. "It's Jake. I've got to take it. Give me a minute."

She nodded, her mouth dry with what she was about to do. The nausea that had been with her since Wayne called was even worse now that she'd made her decision.

"Yeah. I'm at her house now. Okay. We'll be there in an hour. See you then." Cade's voice broke into Piper's thoughts, its hard edge shouting a warning to her nerves.

"Where will we be in an hour?"

He grabbed his plate, set it in the sink, his mouth set in a grim line, a muscle in his jaw clenching with an emotion Piper couldn't name. "Lynchburg police found our tattoo guy early this morning. He was dead. Shot in the head."

The blood drained from Piper's face, and she put a shaky hand to her forehead. "Okay. Now what?"

"Now we go to the county morgue and you identify the tattoo. Make sure it's the one you saw the other night."

Identify the tattoo on the body of a dead man? She shook her head, though she knew she'd do what she'd been asked. "Now?"

"Yeah."

"All right. I'll let Samson out. Then we can leave." She moved by rote, letting the dog outside, calling him in, urging him into his crate. "Be a good boy. I won't be long."

She grabbed her purse, slipped on her shoes, conscious of Cade's gaze, knowing he was worried about her, but unable to think of anything comforting to say.

Finally, when she couldn't put the inevitable off any longer, she grabbed her keys and walked to the door. "Okay. I'm ready."

"Are you?"

"No. I didn't like that tattoo when it was on a living, breathing human being. I'm going to like it even less on a dead body."

"I wish you didn't have to do this, but—"

"But I do. If I don't, we'll never know for sure if this is the right guy, right?"

"It's more than that. We think the guy with the tattoo is a paid thug. Someone hired to come after you. If he is, there will be a connection between him and one of our suspects. Having you identify the tattoo will go a long way in convincing a jury that the thread that connected the deceased and our suspect was also tied to you."

Piper took a deep breath, said a quick prayer that she would be able to do what Cade and Jake were asking, and pulled the front door open. "Then let's go see if it's the same tattoo."

EIGHTEEN

The day was sunny and bright, the sky deep, pure blue. Trees, green with summer growth, shaded the wide road they traveled on. Piper tried to concentrate on those things and not the task before her.

"Are you sure you're okay?" Cade asked.

"Just preparing myself."

"It won't be bad. The medical examiner will have the body covered. All you'll see is the arm."

"A photograph of the arm?"

"I'm afraid not."

"And *I* was afraid you were going to say that." She stared out the window, queasy, nervous, her mind wandering back to the night she'd attended the weight-loss class, to the vitality of the man who'd stared at her from behind the ski mask. Not a nice man, not a good one, but a human being nonetheless. "Did he have a family?"

"Martin? I don't know. Why?"

"I'd hate to think he was a father, a husband, a

son. I'd hate to think people are mourning him, missing him."

"If they are it's because he chose to live his life above the law. If he were alive, he'd be heading to jail, lost to his family just as surely as he is now."

"It's still sad."

"Yeah, it is. But he did it to himself. Someone hired him to kidnap you—"

"We don't know that."

"Sure we do. Think about it. He goes into a room full of witnesses, grabs a woman who looks remarkably like you and tries to drag her outside. Meanwhile, the person who hired him is at a meeting, on a business trip, somewhere far away from Lynchburg with plenty of witnesses of his own who are all willing to testify that he was nowhere near the kidnapping that night."

"The perfect crime?"

"Not even close, but the person who planned it probably thought so. Then, when the composite of the tattoo was released to the press, our guy got scared, thought the kidnapper would get caught and turn state's evidence."

"And decided it was too dangerous to let him live."

"That was his mistake. We're going to get the guy and now he's going to be up on murder one. All we need are a few more pieces of the puzzle."

"Cade?"

"Yeah?" He glanced her way, flashed a dimple by way of encouragement.

Piper had a feeling he wouldn't be smiling when she

told him she'd kept important information to herself for a day. "I got some information yesterday. It's probably nothing, but I think you and Jake should decide."

"Go ahead."

"You know those antiques I've been looking for?"

"Yeah."

"Wayne sold them."

"You found this out yesterday?"

"Yes."

"From who?"

"Wayne."

"And you waited until now to tell me?"

"I wasn't sure it was important. He and Marcus flew to Mexico three times in the past two years. Marcus told us they were vacationing, getting away from things for a while. Wayne told me they were there for experimental treatments. I guess Uncle Marcus didn't think we'd approve."

"And *I* guess it didn't occur to you that Marcus was telling you the truth and that Wayne is the one lying?"

"What reason would he have to lie? All he needed to do was keep silent and I never would have known that he was the one who'd taken those antiques."

"Maybe *you* wouldn't have, but we've been checking with antique dealers since we learned of Wayne's financial situation. Eventually we would have tracked down the missing items and traced the sale to him. He knew that. The story he told you is just a desperate bid to cover up what he's done."

"I don't believe it. Wayne isn't like that." Or was

he? Piper had already learned he wasn't the person she'd imagined him to be, that his past contained dark secrets. Was it really that much of a stretch to believe he'd sell the antiques for personal gain?

"Isn't he? If he's as innocent as he claims, if he sold the antiques to help your uncle, why did it take him this long to admit it?"

"He said…" But suddenly Wayne's excuse seemed to hold little weight or value.

"What? What did he say to convince you to keep quiet?" Cade cut a glance in her direction, his eyes emerald fire in a face tight with anger.

She couldn't answer, wasn't sure how she'd allowed herself to be talked into being silent. No, that wasn't quite true. She'd done it for friendship, but at what cost? "Nothing very convincing."

"So you kept quiet because…?"

"Wayne and I are friends. I trusted him."

"What about *our* friendship? *I* trusted *you* to keep me informed. So did Grayson. So did Jake." Frustration dripped from his voice, and Piper knew he was right to feel it.

"I'm sorry."

"Yeah. Me, too. If you'd come forward with this information yesterday we could have brought him in for questioning. Then maybe…"

He didn't continue, but Piper knew what he was thinking. That if she hadn't kept silent the guy with the tattoo might still be alive.

She blinked back hot tears, turning to stare out the

window, wishing she could go back to yesterday, make a different choice.

But she couldn't. All she could do was move forward.

She glanced at Cade, saw his jaw was clenched tight, his eyes still flashing with anger. Piper wanted to apologize again, but sorry didn't mean much when a man was dead. By the time they arrived at the county morgue, her head ached from holding back tears, her jaw muscles were tight from tension.

There were several cars parked in front of the long, low building. One of them was Grayson's.

"Your brother is here. I'll walk you in. Then I've got to get going." There was a coldness to his voice that Piper hadn't heard before, and she wanted to reach out, touch his arm, see if she could break through the silence between them.

He pulled open the door, and she maneuvered out of the car. "Cade."

"Yes?"

"I really am sorry."

His expression didn't soften, but he reached out to tuck a strand of hair behind her ear. "I know."

Then he pushed open the door to the building and ushered her inside.

An hour and a half later, Piper was home again, a cold compress lying against her eyes, her head resting on her pillow, her legs stretched across the couch.

"Feeling better?" Gray's voice drifted into the

silence and she lifted the compress from her eyes. Her head still throbbed with pain, her stomach twisting in knots. Worse was her brother's concern, his eyes dark with worry, his expression grim.

"No." She dropped the compress back into place, blocking out her brother, the room, Samson lying in a heap on the floor.

Hands wrapped around her ankles as Gray lifted her feet and sat down, then let her feet drop onto his lap. "You did a good job today."

"Good job? I nearly passed out. You had to carry me outside."

"You did good. So, I'm wondering why you're so upset. Is it because seeing the guy upset you, or is it because of Cade."

Both. But that didn't mean she planned to discuss either with her brother. "I'm not upset."

"So why are you hiding behind that rag."

"I'm not hiding."

"Then you won't mind if I do this." He grabbed the compress, pulled it away from her eyes.

"Hey!" She sat up straight, letting her feet drop onto the floor, and started to rise.

Gray grabbed her hand, tugged her back down. "You made a mistake, Piper. It isn't the end of the world."

"It's the end of *his* world."

He didn't ask who she was talking about, just rose and paced across the room.

"Martin made some poor choices. His life would have ended badly, one way or another."

"But if I'd told you about Wayne…"

"Then maybe Martin would have lived a little longer. Maybe. Remember, we don't know for sure that Wayne's done anything wrong."

"That's not what Cade thinks."

"Cade's not thinking straight."

"He—"

"Is angry, disappointed and upset. He'll get over it. The fact is, even if you'd told us about Wayne yesterday we probably couldn't have saved Martin. Without hard evidence we couldn't hold Wayne. He would have been out by early evening. Plenty of time to kill Martin."

"Do you really think that?"

"Yeah, I do. And so does Cade."

"I still wish I'd told you. If I had, maybe things would be different."

"That's your problem, Piper, you always think that if you do a little more, try a little harder, everything will work out perfectly. But it isn't a perfect world. We're not perfect people. We can only do the best we can and pray that God will take care of the rest."

"I know that."

"Do you?"

"Of course I do."

"I wonder." He paced back across the room, leaned against the wall, his face drawn. "You care a lot, Piper. Maybe too much. You've always been that way. When you were a kid you fought for the under-dogs, thought you had to stand up to every bully, be on every committee at school, sell the most candy bars for all the fund-raisers. And it wasn't because you wanted to be the best, or get the awards. It was because you really thought your effort would make a difference."

"There's nothing wrong with that."

"Are you kidding? It's great. I've always wished I could have a little more of your idealism." He smiled, his eyes deep gray and filled with sincerity. "But now you're an adult and I see you doing the same. You don't want people to be hurt, to suffer, to be overburdened, and so you spend an awful lot of time trying to help because you really believe it'll make a difference."

"It *will* make a difference."

He ignored her interruption, just ran a hand along the back of his neck and continued. "The problem is, there's only so much any one of us can do. Sometimes our time is better spent on our knees, praying for those we care about, rather than running around trying to solve problems that are too big for *any* of us to manage."

The words were like a hard punch to the gut, stealing Piper's breath. Not because they were harsh, but because they were true. When was the last time she'd prayed for someone *before* she stepped in and tried to solve the problem? She couldn't remember. Which only made the truth that much harder to bear.

The phone rang and Gray reached over and picked it up before Piper could. "Yeah?" He met her eyes. "This is Grayson. Okay. I'll be there in ten."

"What's going on?"

"Jake's got a search warrant for Wayne's house. They're going there while he's still at work. I want to be there."

"Poor Wayne." A tear escaped, and Piper blinked back more.

"There you go again, sis." Gray wiped the tear from her cheek. "Caring too much. Lock the door. Stay inside. I'll call as soon as I know something."

She waited until the door closed behind him. Then lowered her head to her knees, and did what she should have done for Wayne months ago. She prayed.

NINETEEN

The day dragged on endlessly. Grayson called twice. Once around noon, and again at four. The news wasn't good either time. Guns had been taken from Wayne's gun cabinet. The names of antique dealers taken from his files. It was only a matter of time before an arrest was made.

Piper paced across the living room, wanting to do something, help in some way. Only this time, just as Gray had said, the problem was too big, the solution impossible for her to find.

"I know You're in control, Lord. I know You can fix this."

Despite the prayer, despite the knowledge that everything was in God's hands, Piper's heart was still heavy. She knew the reason. Cade. A few days ago she'd been sure that dating was more trouble than it was worth. That *men* were more trouble than they were worth.

Now she wanted nothing more than to know she hadn't ruined what was between her and Cade—that fledgling relationship that skirted the line between friendship and something more.

When the phone rang again, she hurried to answer it. Hoping for some good news. "Hello?"

"Piper? It's Cade." His voice filled her with warmth and relief.

"Hi."

"I've only got a minute. Things are heating up here."

"Have you arrested Wayne yet?"

"Not yet. It's coming, though. You need to be prepared for it."

"I know." Was that why he'd called?

"You doing okay?"

"Yes."

"Gray said you were upset."

"It's hard not to be."

"Well, hang in there." He sounded distracted, and Piper could hear noise in the background, voices, papers rustling. His sigh was audible. "I thought I'd have more time, but I'm being summoned. We'll talk more later."

Would they? Piper couldn't help wondering as she hung up the phone. All the warmth, concern, gentle humor she was used to from Cade had been missing from the conversation.

Yet another thing she couldn't fix.

Another thing to hand over to God.

There was relief at the thought, at the sure knowledge that God knew what He'd planned for Piper and

Cade, and that nothing she did or didn't do could change that.

For now she'd concentrate on what she could do. She was supposed to meet with Miriam tomorrow. Now was as good a time as any to make sure her information was organized and ready to discuss. First the antique collection file. She opened it, saw the items she'd circled in red. Missing, but now accounted for. She'd deal with that later.

Now the Music Makers files. Her chapter outlines, list of interview dates. *Interviews*. She'd forgotten about the James files. She grabbed her briefcase, pulled out the thick folders. Mr. James had conducted ten interviews before he was killed. Piper read the transcript of each, setting aside several that might be usable. She'd have to call Deborah, tell her that her husband's name would definitely be in the book.

The second folder contained less exciting information. The list of scholarship recipients was the same as one Piper had received from John when she began the book project. She glanced through the pages anyway, noting the highlighted names and the check marks, which must have indicated completed interviews. Mr. James's own personal system of organization.

It made him more real, the need to include his interviews in her book more compelling. On the third page a note was scrawled in sharp, bold letters—*Call M. Verify*. The name and contact information next to it was highlighted in blue. Not the yellow that had been used before. Which must have meant something to the man who'd marked the page.

Intrigued, Piper looked through the list again. Unlike her list, it was collated alphabetically, not by date of scholarship. Several more names were highlighted in blue. She counted fifteen in all. Some were unusual names, names she should have remembered from the list she'd received, but didn't.

She pulled the file John had given her, searching through it for the scholarship list. Wanting to compare the two. Summer camp programs. Instrument distribution. No scholarship list. Where was it? Obviously not where it was supposed to be.

She reached for the phone, eyeing the clock while she dialed Music Makers. She might just reach John before he left for the day.

"John Sweeny."

"Hi, Mr. Sweeny. It's Piper Sinclair."

"How are you, my dear?"

"Fine, thanks. You?" She tapped her fingers against her desk.

"Good. Good. Any news on your attacker?"

Did he know about Wayne's imminent arrest? If not, she didn't plan to be the one to break the news. "Not yet."

"Too bad. You'd think they'd have something to go on by now."

"They're working hard, doing everything they can."

"Yes, well, I admit to some disappointment with

their progress, but that's just between you and me. What can I do for you?"

"I'm embarrassed to admit this, but I've misplaced the list of scholarship recipients you gave me. I was wondering if you could e-mail me a copy."

He was silent for a moment, and Piper wondered if he were going to lecture her on organizational skills. "Hmm. I'd like to, but we've been hit by a virus. The system is down."

"That's okay, then. How about I swing by your office tomorrow and pick it up?"

"I can just as easily come by your house with a copy of it tonight. I'm meeting a friend at the marina anyway. Lee Johnson's fiftieth birthday and he's having the party on a boat, of all things."

"I heard it's going to be the event of the summer."

"If Lee's wife has her way it will be."

"Sounds like fun."

"If you like that kind of thing. I've got to be there by seven, so I'll just make a copy of the list and drop it off before I go."

"I wouldn't want to put you out."

"Don't think another thing about it. I'll see you around six."

He was there by quarter of, driving a car Piper had never seen before, and wearing blue jeans, a dark sweatshirt, oversize sunglasses and a baseball cap.

Piper pulled open the door, smiling as John made his way up the steps. "You're looking very casual today, Mr. Sweeny."

"There's no sense going on a lake dressed in a business suit." His face was flushed, a sheen of sweat on his forehead.

"New car?"

John glanced back at the sporty vehicle, shrugged. "Borrowed from a friend while mine is in the shop."

He stepped into the house, saw Samson rushing toward him and froze. "What is that?"

"My dog. Samson."

"I had no idea you had a dog."

"He's a new addition to the family."

"I see." John's face had flushed bright red, rivulets of sweat dripping down his temples.

"If he makes you uncomfortable, I could put him in my office."

"Thank you. Yes. That would be best." He stepped toward the couch where the James file lay, picked it up and thumbed through it, his gaze still on the dog.

"Come on, Sam."

The big dog sat on his haunches and refused to budge, eyeing John with an angry glower that only made the man more nervous.

"Samson! Come!"

Finally, reluctantly, Samson moved, walking into the office with Piper and whining as she closed the door behind him.

"May I ask what you're working on?" He'd come up behind her so silently Piper nearly jumped out of her skin when he spoke.

She whirled around, her heart beating a little too

hard and a little too fast, saw the James file in his hand. "Just organizing information for my meeting with Miriam tomorrow."

She stepped around him, heading for the living room, wanting to put distance between them and not sure why.

"This is the information you received from Mrs. James, isn't it?" He was close again, and Piper turned to face him, alarms screaming through her mind.

"Part of it. The rest is in my office. Would you like to see it? I can get it—" She started back down the hall, and he pulled her up short, his hand tight around her arm.

"No. No. Don't bother. We wouldn't want to let the dog out again."

"Right. So, you brought the file?"

"A wasted effort. You won't be needing it."

That didn't sound good, but Piper pasted a smile on her face anyway, tugging her arm from his grip, moving toward the front door. "You're probably right. I'll just give Miriam what I have. She'll be pleased. The book is coming together beautifully."

"Yes. The book. A mistake to allow Miriam to even entertain the idea. But how could I have known things would go this far? And the James woman? She couldn't leave well enough alone." He was rambling, speaking more to himself than Piper, his eyes wild as he reached for her again.

She dodged, the crutch slipping on the wood floor, her leg going out from under her. She caught her balance on the door, gasping as John's hand dug into her shoulder, the still raw wound searing with pain. "What's going on, Mr. Sweeny? What's wrong?"

"Nothing. Nothing. Just a loose end to tie up. I didn't want to. Not at all. I tried every way I could to keep from having to hurt you. But you're as stubborn and tenacious as your uncle." He pulled something from his pocket, slammed it into Piper's upper arm.

There was a sting of pain. A moment of understanding, and then she was falling. The world going black around her.

The call came in at 11:00 p.m. Cade was outside the interrogation room, listening as Jake questioned Wayne, when his cell phone rang.

He grabbed it, not even bothering to look at the caller ID, sure it was his father calling to complain about something. "Yeah."

"Piper's missing." Grayson. His voice harsh, abrupt.

Cade's heart stalled, started again. "Are you sure?"

"Do you think I'd call if I weren't? I'm at her house. She's gone. The car isn't. The dog's gone, too. Looks like he went through the office window. There's blood on the glass. Get someone out here. Now." He hung up.

Cade strode into the interrogation room, met Jake's startled gaze. "Piper's missing. Do what you need to do here. I'm heading to her house."

TWENTY

Dark. Hot. Cramped. Pain. Those were the things Piper noticed as she came to. Her knee throbbed, her shoulder screamed in protest. A gag kept her from calling out, bonds of some sort held her wrists and ankles together. She was upright, but hunched over, her head pressed close down against her knees, her chest heaving to bring in more air. She tried to move, felt a trickle of blood slide down her back.

Where was she? A box of some sort? A coffin? The thought filled her with terror, and she rocked her weight back and forth trying to shift the prison that held her. It moved. A slight shift, a soft thump.

So she wasn't buried underground. She'd have to keep wiggling, keep trying, until she forced the box open or loosened her bonds.

Minutes later she was light-headed with effort and sticky with sweat or blood. She wasn't sure which. Not that it mattered. The heat was suffocating, the pressure of her head pressed against her knee making it difficult to breath. She gasped for air, trying to calm her racing heart. Trying to think.

John. How could it be that a man she'd known for most of her life could have fooled her so easily? Fooled everyone who knew and respected him? Fooled Marcus.

Or had he? John had wanted the James file. Obviously it contained information dangerous to him. An image flashed through Piper's mind—blue highlighted names, a note to verify information. She'd been over her own list countless times, calling people, setting up interviews. She'd recognize most of the names if she saw them again. And, yet, not one of the blue highlighted names sounded familiar.

Why not?

Because they weren't on her list. Because the people they belonged to didn't exist.

Puzzle pieces slid into place—the kidnapping attempt a few days before she was scheduled to go to Richmond, John's offer to retrieve the files, the door to the bungalow opened when she'd thought she had closed it. Then the attacks on her life. One after another, as if someone were becoming more and more desperate.

And of course, John *had* been desperate.

He'd needed to either retrieve the list of recipients Marcus had given to Mr. James, or stop Piper from comparing it to the one John had provided her. Otherwise, it was only a matter of time before Piper discovered the discrepancies and started asking questions. Questions that would prove very difficult for John to answer.

How long had he been embezzling funds from Music Makers? And what was the extent of the damage? Thousands of dollars? Hundreds of thousands? Had Marcus known?

Of course he had.

He'd provided the scholarship list to Mr. James in good faith, believing the information accurate. Piper could imagine his frustration and worry when he was called and asked to verify not just one set of names and contact information, but many.

Had he called John? Expressed his concern? Asked his best friend and business partner to conduct an internal audit?

Probably. He'd have had no reason to doubt his friend's honesty. Though he might have doubted Wayne, might have wondered if his stepson were skimming money from Music Makers by creating phony scholarship recipients.

Had John murdered Marcus to keep his secret safe? Had he murdered Mr. James?

More puzzle pieces, all fitting so well together that the picture they created couldn't be denied.

Of course he'd murdered them. Or had them murdered. Based on his means of disposing of Piper, she could only assume that he didn't have the stomach to actually murder someone himself. No, he'd just let her die a slow, horrible death.

Or maybe not.

Maybe he'd left her here until he could come back and dispose of her more effectively.

Another picture flashed through Piper's mind—a pale arm, a snake tattoo, specks of blood on the sheet that shrouded the rest of the body.

No, John definitely didn't have a problem killing people. So maybe he'd meet his friends at the marina, then come back to finish what he'd started.

But not if she could escape first.

How much time did she have? How long had she been unconscious?

Sweat trickled down Piper's face, wetting the knees of her sweatpants. She tried to move again, tried to work past the feeling that she was suffocating and force her body to contort enough so that she could force the gag away from her mouth. At least if she could do that she could call for help, try to get someone's attention.

If there was anyone near enough to hear.

"Nothing." Frustration and anger made Cade's voice sharp. "No sign of a forced entry. No evidence of a struggle."

"Scratches on the door are interesting." Jake stood near the office door, eying the deep gouges on it.

"The dog. It has to be. She must have locked him in here. And he wanted out bad enough to go through the window." Grayson looked haggard, black stubble on his jaw only accentuating his pallor.

"No one's seen him?" This from Jake, who

surveyed the room with a critical eye, perhaps looking for something Cade had missed, some clue that might lead to Piper.

Cade only wished he would find one. "No. The guy next door did see a car parked in front of her house. Said it was blue or black, but Piper has so many people come for piano lessons he didn't pay much attention."

"He know how long the car was out there?"

"Not long. He watched a half hour of news, looked back out the window and it was gone. He didn't see the dog. Didn't notice the broken window."

"So we've got nothing. I need to call my family. I need to let them know what's going on. Get them all praying." Grayson walked out of the room, his shoulders slumped, the truth that none of them would speak a heavy weight—forty-eight hours. That's all they had. If they didn't find her by then, they probably never would.

"What time?" Jake's question drew Cade away from his worries.

"What?"

"What time was the car outside?"

"Around six."

Jake glanced at his watch. Frowned. "So we've already lost almost six hours."

"Yeah."

"We've ruled out Wayne. Ruled out Brian. Guy with the tattoo is dead. Who does that leave us with?"

"Someone who knew Piper. Someone who's affiliated with Music Makers. Someone she trusts enough to let into her house." Cade's jaw clenched as he pictured Piper smiling, opening the door, letting her enemy in.

"Someone who knew enough about Wayne to set him up."

"Which would mean someone privy to very private information. Someone Marcus might have shared financial information with…" His voice trailed off, his eyes meeting Jake's. "John Sweeny."

"He fits."

"Then let's go find him."

Jake's cell phone rang as they walked out of the house. "Reed. Yeah. Sounds like him. We'll be there in ten."

"What?"

"There's a dog making a racket out near Wayne's place. Neighbors called animal control to complain."

"Samson?"

"Sounds like it."

"Where?"

"Lakeshore Drive."

"I'm going." Cade strode toward his car, Jake beside him.

"And I'll go have a talk with Mr. Sweeny."

TWENTY-ONE

The moon shone high and bright, a yellow orb in the midnight sky. Cade parked behind the animal control van and stepped out into humid air, praying the dog was Samson and that Piper was somewhere nearby.

And that she was alive.

He'd planned to stop by her house in the morning, make sure she was okay, tell her he was sorry for leaving her at the morgue. Duty had called, but so had anger. He'd wanted her to trust him, to count on him. When she hadn't, he'd been angry. Now he regretted it.

Was it too late?

He didn't want to believe it, but his years as a crime-scene photographer told him otherwise. He'd seen too many bodies, too many wounded and dying people, to not know the depth of human depravity. Piper had been a threat to someone. The end result just might be her death.

A dog howled somewhere close by, a high, mournful cry. Cade strode toward the sound, walking through a grove of trees and down toward the lake. The water shone black as ink, flashes of light, voices, a deep growl drawing Cade forward.

A crowd had formed near the edge of the lake— a uniformed officer, two people from animal control holding catch poles, several civilians dressed in shorts, others in pajamas and slippers—all watching the dog that paced in front of an oversize shed.

"You Officer Macalister?" A tall, leggy redhead stepped toward him, her skin pale in the moonlight.

"That's right."

"Tori Riley. I'm a vet. Animal control called me to tranquilize the dog, but Sheriff Reed asked me to wait until you got here. You know the animal?"

Did he? The growling, barking animal in front of him looked nothing like the silly, sloppy dog Piper had adopted. "Samson?"

The dog cocked his head, stared hard at Cade, then barked again.

"Yeah. I know him. His owner is missing."

"So we were told. He's guarding that shed like it's a two-ton rawhide bone. Your guy wants in there, but the dog won't let him near it."

"Let me try." He stepped forward, held a hand out. "What's going on, Samson? Where's Piper?"

The dog sniffed his fingers, licked his hand and sat down in front of the shed's door.

"You gonna let me get in there?" He nudged Samson with his foot, pulled at the door. It was locked. Cade slammed the heel of his foot into the old wood, adrenaline, worry, anger adding strength to the movement. The wood splintered, and he peered into a dark, cavernous space. "Piper?"

Nothing. Not a sound. Not a breath.

"Here." Someone thrust a flashlight toward him and he flashed it inside the stifling space. Tools, boxes, a few old wooden trunks. Nothing he wouldn't expect in a shed this size. He pointed the flashlight toward the floor, saw dust and debris.

Was that a footprint?

"See anything?" Grayson was beside him, out of breath, panting, energy and anger flowing off him in waves.

"I'm not sure. Piper?"

Still nothing. If she was in there she was unconscious, or couldn't speak. Or worse.

He wouldn't think that. Wouldn't believe it.

Someone was calling her name. Piper heard it through a haze of pain. Her muscles cramped, her lungs straining, she wanted out of her prison badly enough to imagine rescue.

Please God, get me out of here.

The prayer whispered through her mind. Not the first, but perhaps the most desperate. It wasn't death that she feared at the moment, but the slow torture of hours or days spent in the trap that held her.

How long would she survive? And which would be destroyed first? Her body or her mind?

At the rate thing were going, Piper was beginning to suspect she'd lose her mind before her body succumbed. First she'd thought she'd heard a dog howling. Now she was sure she heard voices.

But, of course, that was impossible. Wasn't it?

"Piper!" This time she was sure of what she heard. Grayson's voice, raw, worried. And close.

She tried to move, but her muscles were useless, her circulation cut off. The most she could manage was a muffled moan. Not enough to draw attention. Not enough to save her.

Something bumped into her prison. A dog barked, scratched a paw against the outside of the box. Then more thumping, frantic voices. The chest she was in moved, jerking up a little before settling back down. "This is it. She's in here."

The box shimmied, slid, and then the top popped open, musty air wafted over her and light illuminated her prison. She wanted to lift her head, but her body refused to obey the command, refusing even the most simple of movements.

A hand slid beneath her hair, feeling for the pulse point at her neck, the touch gentle, almost a caress. "She's alive. Call an ambulance. Piper, can you hear me?" Cade spoke close to her ear, fear beneath the words.

She mumbled against the gag, used all her strength to turn her head toward him. His eyes were deep green and swimming with emotion. "Thank God. I thought we'd lost you. Stay still. I'm going to get you out of there."

He put his hands under her arms, pulled her up and

out, supporting her weight, not releasing his hold even as he shifted his grip, wrapped his arms around her waist. "Gray, get the gag off. Ms. Riley, can you untie her ankles?"

The gag loosened, and Piper winced as it pulled away from her skin. "John Sweeny." She managed to rasp out the words, her throat so dry and parched she thought she'd be sick.

"Jake is already on the way to question him." Cade's words were terse, his touch tender as he smoothed hair away from her damp face.

"He's been embezzling funds from Music Makers. I think he killed my uncle."

"We'll sort it all out."

"And the writer who was doing the human interest story on Marcus and Music Makers. I think John killed him, too. I think he found out that some of the scholarship recipients were phony—"

"Shhhh." Cade put a finger over her lips, sealing in words that begged for escape. "We'll sort it out, but let's get you to the hospital first." He untied her wrists, rubbed her hands as blood flooded back into them.

"How are you doing, Piper?" A red-haired woman Piper recognized, but whose name she couldn't remember, peered into her eyes.

"I'm okay."

"An ambulance is on the way." Grayson moved close, brushed a hand against her forehead. "You're too hot. We need to get her outside, Cade."

"Right."

One minute she was standing, the next she was floating, carried in strong arms out into balmy night air. Then laid on a blanket of soft grass.

"Hey, you still with us?" Cade bent over her, his face lined with concern.

"Where else would I be?"

He chuckled, shook his head. "I think you're going to make it."

"I'd better. Someone's got to take care of Samson. He's a hero. I guess God knew what He was doing when He put the two of us together."

"He knew what He was doing when He put the two of *us* together, too."

"Cade—"

"I was an idiot yesterday. I should never have left you when you were so upset."

"It wasn't a big deal."

"Wasn't it? We're building something together, Piper, something special. You can't tell me you don't feel it."

"No, I can't."

"Then you can't tell me that what I did didn't hurt you."

"It doesn't matter."

"*You* matter. A lot." He took her hand, curved his fingers around hers. "Forgive me?"

She nodded, swallowing back tears of relief, and of happiness.

"Good." He leaned down, brushed a kiss against her lips.

Grayson cleared his throat, squeezed Piper's other hand. "The ambulance is here. I'm going to flag them down."

"And I'm going to call Jake, see if John is in custody yet."

Piper tightened her grip on Cade's hand. "He was supposed to be at a party on the lake."

"I'll tell Jake."

"I think he planned to come back and kill me. He could be on the way here now." She levered up, her heart beating faster, fear clawing at her stomach.

"He won't get within a mile of you. We know who we're looking for, now. There's nowhere John can hide, nowhere he can go that we won't find him. So relax. Let Jake, Grayson and me take care of it."

A month ago Piper would have tried to find a way to be involved, sure that her effort would make everything work out. But she'd learned something valuable in the last few days; learned that even her best efforts couldn't solve every problem, and that sometimes the best thing she could do was wait in silence and prayer for others to do what she couldn't.

She relaxed back down onto the ground, staring up at the sky, the stars, the bright moon. Listening to Cade's voice as he spoke to Jake, the ambulance sirens, Samson's gentle huffs of breath, the beat of her own heart.

This was what life was about. Here. Now. Not the future. The great plan. The goals. But enjoying the moments. The seconds. The chances. Open and willing for whatever God would bring her way.

Even if that was a strong-willed, determined man who'd annoy her to no end, but who would always have her back, always want the best for her and always point her in the right direction when she got off track.

She turned to look at Cade, tugging his hand toward her, pressing a kiss to his knuckles.

He smiled, met her gaze, his voice faltering for just a moment before it strengthened again, his hand curving around hers as he lifted it and pressed it to his heart.

EPILOGUE

"Forget it. I've changed my mind." Piper hiked up her floor-length skirt and pivoted on too-high heels, almost tripping in her haste to return to the limo that idled at the curb. The night, heavy and bleak with winter, was filled with noise and lights as cars were parked and people made their way toward the museum.

"You can't change your mind." Gabby hissed the words, grabbing Piper's arm and pulling her to a stop. "You've planned this for months. There are three hundred and fifty people waiting to see you."

"Not me. The exhibit. And I'm not changing my mind about attending. I'm changing my mind about wearing this dress while I do it. I can't believe I let you talk me into it." She grabbed a handful of royal blue silk and frowned. "It's so…"

"Elegant?"

"That wasn't quite the word I was looking for."

"Well, it should have been."

"Maybe. But it's not me. I'm more the jeans and T-shirt type."

"I bet Cade would disagree with that."

"With what?" Cade's voice was warm, smooth honey, sliding down Piper's spine and calming the nerves that had been gnawing at her for the better part of the day.

She swung to face him, her heart soaring as she met his gaze. "You made it!"

"I told you I'd be here." He opened his arms and she flew into them, her high heels no longer the problem they'd been moments before.

He felt good—solid, warm, familiar—and she wrapped her arms around his waist, pulling him close. "I missed you."

"I missed you, too. The next time I go on an out-of-state photo shoot, I'll have to bring you with me."

Piper eased back, looked up into his eyes. "Logan Airport has been closed since early this morning. I thought you were stuck in Massachusetts."

"And miss the grand opening of the exhibit? No way. I rented a car as soon as I heard the weather report yesterday afternoon. Hit some snow on the way down, but nothing too bad."

"I can't believe you drove all the way here." She hugged him again, only loosening her grip when Gabby cleared her throat and tapped on Piper's shoulder.

"I hate to interrupt the reunion, but we really should go inside."

"You're right." Cade grabbed Piper's hand. "Let's go. And while we're walking, one of you can tell me what it is I wouldn't agree with."

"Piper says she's a jeans and T-shirt kind of gal. I said I didn't think you'd agree. Especially not when you saw her in that dress."

Cade's gaze swept from Piper's professionally styled hair, down the length of blue silk that fell against the curves of her body and back up to meet her eyes. "No. You are definitely *not* a jeans and T-shirt kind of gal. You look gorgeous."

"So do you." And he did, the tuxedo he wore perfectly fitted, his hair brushing against the collar of his jacket, his eyes vivid green and bright with warmth.

"Enough already. You're making goo-goo eyes at each other. Don't you know how seventh-grade that is?" Gabby's words dripped with disgust, though Piper knew her friend was happy that Cade had arrived.

"You're just irritable because you haven't seen Wayne today." Piper's teasing words brought a blush to Gabby's cheeks.

It was still there as they stepped inside the museum's front doors, the pink flush adding delicate color to her skin.

People milled about, talking, chatting and laughing as they waited for the doors to the exhibit to open. Several waved and called hello as Piper made her way through the room. She waved back, but didn't stop to chat. She was too nervous, too afraid the hard work that had gone into creating the exhibit and the Music Makers commemorative book would prove to have been a waste, the results lackluster and the anticipated donations a letdown.

"Everything is wonderful, so stop frowning." Cade's words were soft, meant only for Piper, and he gave her hand a gentle squeeze.

"I'm just nervous."

"Don't be. Miriam let me walk through the exhibit earlier. It's phenomenal."

"The book is wonderful, too. The pictures, the stories. You did such a great job." Gabby spoke up, her gaze scanning the room. "Hey, there's Wayne! Let's go say hello."

Piper wasn't sure that was a good idea. Though Wayne tolerated Gabby's fawning attention, he didn't seem nearly as interested in spending time with her as she was in spending time with him. Though, in all fairness, Wayne's time was limited. John's arrest had created a gap in Music Makers. One Wayne had been determined to fill. His familiarity with the company's finances and his vision for building a fiscally stronger organization had led the board of directors to unanimously agree to name him CEO. Since then, Wayne had been working at a fevered pitch, determined to undo the damage John's embezzlement schemes had done to Music Makers' reputation. Only time would tell if that effort would pay off.

At least the financial burden he'd carried was gone, Marcus's life insurance more than enough to cover the debt. What was left, Wayne had put into rebuilding Music Makers, a move that had endeared him to the community and to the board of directors.

"Hey, you still with us?" Cade whispered in Piper's ear as Gabby hurried to Wayne's side.

"Where else would I be?"

"Lost in your memories."

Piper shook her head and tried to smile. "Not tonight. Tonight is about the future."

"That's exactly what I was thinking. There's just one problem."

"What's that?" Piper looked around, trying to spot trouble.

"Your outfit."

"I thought you said I looked gorgeous."

"You do, but there's something missing."

She glanced down at the dress. "What?"

"A flower."

"A *flower?*"

"For your hair. And I know just where to find one." He tugged her toward the door that led into the exhibit.

"You're kidding, right? We've been going out for months, have known each other since we were kids, and you think I'd wear a flower in my hair?" She wasn't sure if she should be amused or exasperated.

"Humor me." He smiled at Miriam, who was standing outside the door, ready to hand out programs and greet patrons. "Mind if we go in a few minutes early, Miriam?"

"Not at all." She pushed the door open, and Cade pulled Piper across the threshold.

The exhibit was stunning, the instruments and antiquities displayed to the best advantage, each piece with a unique history. Piper would have spent time wandering through the exhibit rooms, but Cade had other ideas and hurried her along.

"Can we slow down? These heels aren't easy to run in."

"Sorry. I forgot you're handicapped tonight." He flashed a grin, pushed a door open and stepped back so Piper could walk in.

It was a small room. Not part of the exhibit and empty but for an antique table and a crystal vase that overflowed with roses—pink, yellow, red—their heady aroma filling the room.

"Wow!" Piper leaned forward and inhaled deeply.

Cade pulled one from the arrangement. "Red will look great in your hair."

"We can't just take one. That would be stealing. You're a police officer. You know better."

"A reservist. I'm not on active duty. Besides, the flowers are yours."

"They are?" The anxiety and stress of the exhibit's opening night faded away, replaced by warmth and love. "Cade, they're gorgeous! Thank you."

"I wanted to surprise you, but couldn't decide which color best suited our relationship—yellow for friendship, pink for love, red for passion."

"So, you got them all." Piper took the red rose he'd offered. "They're so beautiful. How could I not want to wear one in my hair?"

He laughed, shook his head. "I was kidding. I don't really expect you to wear one. You look stunning just the way you are. Nothing could add to the beauty I see when I look at you." The laughter was gone, his gaze solemn and filled with emotion.

Piper's breath caught, her heart beating slow and heavy. "That's the most romantic thing anyone has ever said to me."

"Is it?" He leaned toward her, captured her lips with his. "Then I guess I don't need to say the rest."

"The rest?"

"The rest of what I've been practicing for the past twenty-four hours."

"I'd hate for you to waste all that effort. Go ahead. Say it."

"Okay, let's see if I can get this right. When I look at you, I'm reminded of the past—of being a kid, of laughter, of joy, of innocence." He took her hand, squeezed it. "And I'm reminded of the present—that today is what we have, a gift from God, one we should cherish and enjoy. Even more, when I look at you, I'm reminded that the future is what we make it, that God gives us gifts, strengths, blessings and those things travel with us as we move through life. You are one of those gifts and I will always treasure you."

Piper swallowed past a lump in her throat, her eyes cloudy with unshed tears as she threw her arms around him. "I can't believe you just said that. Has your dad been coaching you again?"

"No, this time I came up with it all on my own." He rested his cheek against the top of her head. "I love you, Piper."

"I love you, too."

"Then maybe you won't mind adding something besides a flower to your outfit." He eased back, pulled a small jeweler's box from his pocket. Inside, lying on a bed of satin, was the most beautiful ring Piper had ever seen—a sapphire surrounded by diamonds and set in platinum.

Piper's breath caught again, her slow-beating heart picking up speed. "Cade…"

"I thought about getting something more traditional, but a little color seemed more your style."

More her style? Any style would be hers if it meant what she thought it meant.

Cade lifted her hand, kissed her knuckles. "I was going to wait until we'd dated a year, but I didn't need a year to know what I wanted. I'm hoping you want the same. Will you marry me, Piper?"

"If I say yes do I get to keep the ring?" The words escaped on a nervous breath, and Cade laughed.

"If it fits." He slipped the ring on her finger.

Like Cade, it fit perfectly.

Piper lifted her hand, watching as the sapphire and diamonds caught the light. "It's perfect, Cade, but I need to know one more thing."

"What's that?"

"Do I get to keep you?"

"Forever."

"Then, yes, I'll marry you."

He smiled and claimed her lips once again.

* * * * *

Dear Reader,

Life is noisy kids, spouses, friends, jobs, all vying for our attention. Add to that the roar of traffic, the lilting music from the radio, the dramatic overtones of the television, and the noise becomes almost deafening. With our modern lives so filled with demands, it's easy to be swept along on the waves of sound, carried here and there in ever more frantic motion.

A few years ago, during one of the most hectic times in my life, I visited Smith Mountain Lake with my husband and kids. Early one morning, before the rest of my clan woke, I stepped outside. Water rippled against the shore and fish splashed in the lake, but other than that the world was silent. During those few moments of precious solitude I realized I'd been so busy, so caught up in the noisy demands of life, I'd forgotten how important it is to sit in silence and to listen.

Piper Sinclair is like that, so caught up in her busy life she's forgotten that talking to God requires tuning in and waiting for the quiet stirring of the soul that says—"Yes, you're on the right track" or "Come on, kid, get it together." When Piper's life is threatened and her busy world becomes chaotic and unpredictable, she must learn that taking the time to wait for God's answer is as important as rushing to meet life's demands.

Join Piper and photographer Cade Macalister as they work to stop a person bent on destruction, and when you're finished, drop me a line. I can be reached by mail at 1121 Annapolis Road, PMB 244, Odenton, Maryland, 21113-1633. Or by e-mail at shirlee@shirleemccoy.com.

Blessings,

Shirlee McCoy

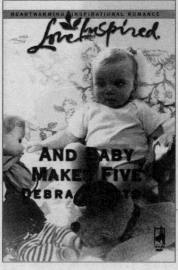

2 Love Inspired novels and a mystery gift... Absolutely FREE!

Visit
www.LoveInspiredBooks.com
for your two FREE books, sent directly to you!

BONUS: Choose between regular print or our NEW larger print format!

There's no catch! You're under no obligation to buy anything. We charge nothing—ZERO—for your first shipment. And you don't have to make any minimum number of purchases.

You'll like the convenience of home delivery at our special discount prices, and you'll love your free subscription to Steeple Hill News, our members-only newsletter.

We hope that after receiving your free books, you'll want to remain a subscriber. But the choice is yours—to continue or cancel, anytime at all! So why not take us up on our invitation, with no risk of any kind!

Love Inspired